CAPE COD SEAL RESCUE

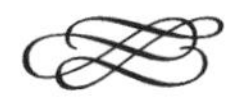

ELLE JAMES

CAPE COD SEAL RESCUE

BROTHERHOOD PROTECTORS SERIES
BOOK #10

New York Times & USA Today
Bestselling Author

Elle James

EBOOK ISBN: 978-1-62695-169-3

PRINT ISBN: 978-1-62695-170-9

AUTHOR'S NOTE

Enjoy other military books by Elle James

Brotherhood Protectors Series

Montana SEAL (#1)
Bride Protector SEAL (#2)
Montana D-Force (#3)
Cowboy D-Force (#4)
Montana Ranger (#5)
Montana Dog Soldier (#6)
Montana SEAL Daddy (#7)
Montana Ranger's Wedding Vow (#8)
Montana SEAL Undercover Daddy (#9)
Cape Cod SEAL Rescue (#10)
Montana SEAL Friendly Fire (#11)
Montana SEAL's Bride (#11) TBD
Montana Rescue
Hot SEAL, Salty Dog

Visit ellejames.com for more titles and release dates
For hot cowboys, visit her alter ego Myla Jackson
at mylajackson.com
and join Elle James and Myla Jackson's Newsletter
at Newsletter

Thank you to all my lovely readers who make my dreams come true by buying my books, thus allowing me to continue to write stories. You are wonderful!

Escape with...

Elle James

CHAPTER 1

"WHAT'S the real reason for your visit to the Cape, Hank?" John Decker turned the glass of whiskey around in the pool of condensation on the bar and stared into the clear amber liquid. "And don't tell me you want to recruit me for the Brotherhood Protectors. I'm not a retired war hero."

Hank Patterson sat beside him on a bar stool in the Gone Fishin' Bar & Grill overlooking the beach. "You know why. I couldn't let you celebrate your Alive Day alone."

Decker's chest tightened. Each year, he worked hard to make his heart numb to the so-called celebration of his Alive Day. The day his world had ended. "I keep telling you, I'd rather let the day pass. I've never felt like celebrating the day, and think it's pretty damned insensitive of you to bring it up each year." He lifted his glass, drained the last of his scotch and returned the glass to the bar with a little more force than necessary. Then he turned to face one of the only friends he had left. "What's to celebrate, anyway? Allison died that day."

"Decker, your Alive Day is the day you lived after an accident that very nearly took your life." Hank's gaze captured Decker's. "You're alive."

"And Allison is dead," Decker repeated. "She died because of me."

"You didn't make the other driver crash into you."

"No, but I could have reacted faster. I shouldn't have been arguing with Allison over going to visit her mother. It's my fault I wasn't paying close enough attention to the oncoming traffic. If I had, I might have swerved in time to miss the other car."

Hank drummed his fingers on the counter, his jaw tightening. "Or you might have run off the road, flipped your car and landed upside down in a ditch filled with water from the recent rain, and you both would have been dead."

"Sometimes I wish that had been the case," Decker muttered. He leaned across the bar and motioned to Roxi, the bartender who was yet another reminder of his guilt. "Can I get another?"

Roxi Lanier smiled, her blue eyes twinkling. With a nod, her blond hair spilled over her shoulder in long luxurious waves. "Scotch on the rocks, coming in just a minute." She tossed her head back, flinging her mane of hair behind her, exposing her light blue Gone Fishin' tank top, the uniform of the bar she owned and operated.

Decker liked when Roxi smiled. It cheered him when he was at his lowest.

He didn't need another scotch. He rarely drank anymore. He'd only ordered it as a diversion from his conversation with Hank. The diversion wouldn't last long if he knew the man as well as he thought he did. A busy man since he'd established the Brotherhood Protectors, Hank rarely ventured out of Montana. But when he did, it was for a purpose. This time he'd left his wife, ranch and business to see Decker through the anniversary of his wife's death.

The two friends had met while serving as US Navy SEALs. Hank had left the Navy before Decker to help his father on his ranch in Montana. Decker had left the Navy after the accident, that had taken his wife's life, had caused him to be medically discharged from the military.

When Hank opened his mouth to say something, Decker raised a hand to stop him before he got started. "If you want to be a *real* friend, you won't keep showing up on the anniversary of Allison's death. It's not like I don't have enough reminders already." His mother had called that morning to check on him. His married sister had taken the time out of her day to call that evening to make sure he wasn't contemplating putting a gun to his head. "The thing to remember is that I'm fine."

"Then why don't you come back to Montana with me?"

Decker shook his head. "I don't fit in out there. I'm not a cowboy or a bodyguard. I would never fit into your protection business."

"Then buy a business, get a job in a firm using your engineering degree, or teach fly fishing. Do something that gets you involved with other people."

"Thanks to a friend who suggested I try life on Cape Cod, I've discovered the latent beach bum in me. I like it here and I don't see any reason to return to the rat race when I can telecommute from paradise."

Hank snorted. "You've only been here for a summer. The winters can be pretty brutal on the Cape."

"I can handle anything the weather can throw at me. And despite what my mother and sister think, I'm not falling apart."

"I'm glad to hear that." Hank's lips quirked. "Your mother is a power to be reckoned with. I'm surprised she didn't come to the Cape to supervise your Alive Day herself."

"She had a date."

Hank's brows rose. "Good for her."

Decker shuddered. "Seems strange—my mother going out on a date." His father's death five years ago had left his mother spinning. Kind of like him when Allison died.

"She's getting on with her life," Hank said. "Which is more than I can say for you."

"I moved to the coast. How much more *getting on with my life* does everyone expect?"

"Since you've been here—no, since the accident—how many dates have you been on?" Hank asked.

Decker glanced toward Roxi, hoping she'd come with his drink and give him an excuse not to answer the question. Concentrating on the pretty bartender was easier than dealing with his wreck of a life. "I'm not ready to date." He wasn't sure he'd ever be ready to date again. And not from a lack of available women who'd been all over the island during the summer months.

"You need to get back into the swing of things," Hank said. "You're young, with your whole life ahead of you. Surely there were women swarming all over the Cape this summer. Didn't you find even one of them interesting?"

Since his house was right on the beach, every time he sat out on the deck, he'd had women in skimpy bikinis show up, asking for directions. Or they'd want to know whether or not he had any sunscreen he could smooth over their bodies, each in a blatant attempt to draw him out of the shadows and into a summer fling. He'd sent them on their way, not in the least interested in starting something he had no intention of finishing. Not one of the summer beach babes had inspired a pressing need to get closer to establish intimacy. He'd been celibate so long, he wasn't sure he was attracted to women anymore.

Except maybe one.

Roxi bent to retrieve a bottle from beneath the counter, her cutoff shorts rising up the backs of her thighs, exposing more than a little of the curve of her golden-tanned ass.

A spark of desire sent an electric jolt straight to his groin. Hell. He'd been having more of those lately, every time he came to the Gone Fishin' Bar & Grill, even when he told himself he was only there for the food and drink. He hated the lie he told himself and despised the fact he was even having those feelings for another woman when his wife was dead. He tried to tell himself he shouldn't feel guilty for lusting after another woman. His wife had been gone for two years.

And why Roxi? She's nothing like my wife.

The bartender wasn't twig-thin and delicate like Allison. Roxi had curves. From the firm rise of her breasts beneath the tank top, to the narrow indentation of her waistline and the rounded swells of her hips, she was sexy, shapely and trim. The muscle tone bespoke a more active life than that of just a bartender. He'd seen her wind-surfing and paddle boarding on the water in front of his cottage.

At night when he couldn't sleep, Decker sat on his porch overlooking the ocean. On many occasions he'd caught her walking or jogging along the beach late at night or in the early morning hours. She'd run by with her big German shepherd, her bare feet kicking up sand, long lithe legs glowing a silvery blue in the moonlight.

Decker tore his gaze away from Roxi's backside and stared into his empty glass. Out of the corner of his eye he saw Hank's gaze slide from Roxi and back to him. Damn, Hank had caught him staring at the pretty bartender. Decker cringed. His friend was sure to make something of it.

Hank's eyes narrowed and his lips twisted. "Yeah, it's about time you started dating again."

"Just because you've found someone to love, doesn't mean everyone needs the same. You were perfectly happy being a bachelor until Sadie came along."

A smile slid across Hank's face. "I was, wasn't I? But then, I think I knew what I was missing. And if I couldn't have Sadie, I didn't want anyone else."

"And that's a bad thing?" Decker's gaze slipped to Roxi again. "I like working from the comfort of my beach house."

"Doing what?"

"Odd jobs, some cybersluething. How many people in Little Creek, Virginia do you know who would give their right arm to live my life?"

Hank's lips twisted. "You have a point. But I think I'd feel better about you throwing away your life if you were actually happy here. I guess because I'm happy, I like to see others around me as happy."

"Well, set your mind at ease. I'm *satisfied* with the way I'm living my life." Decker repeated the same words he'd spoken to his mother, hoping the more he reiterated the sentiment, the more truth he'd find in it.

"Yeah." Hank's eyes narrowed. "But it's not lost on me that you didn't say you were happy."

Decker grunted. "Satisfied is as good a word as happy."

Hank shook his head. "You're wrong on that count. When you're happy, you'll know the difference." He clapped a hand on Decker's shoulder. "But I'll quit butting in on your self-proclaimed two-year-long wallowing. It's your life." He stood and stretched. "But I've got to tell you, you're missing so much more."

"We're not all built the same," Decker reminded his friend.

"True." Hank glanced at his watch and winced. "I obviously need more sleep than you do. I'm heading back to my cottage."

Decker lifted his glass. "Say hello to Sadie for me."

Hank stood. "She would have come tonight, but she was busy packing to go back to Montana."

"I'm surprised you talked her into coming out here for the week. I didn't think she'd leave the baby for even that long."

With a twisted smile, Hank said, "Chuck, one of my Brotherhood Protectors, is keeping Emma. Sometimes I think she loves him more than me."

"What about Sadie's acting career?"

"She's on hiatus between sets. The week here was just what she needed."

"I can't get over my buddy Hank, married to a mega-movie star." Decker shook his head. "She's special."

Hank's smile widened. "You only know the half of it. You need to come out to Montana and meet Emma. That kid has us wrapped around her little pinky."

Decker snorted. "Sadie's so much in the public eye. I don't know how you two get along. Do you ever get tired of the publicity?"

Hank's brows furrowed as he considered Decker's comment. Finally, he said, "When she's not in LA, she's at the ranch in Montana. It helps keep both of her lives separate. Besides, Sadie balances me. I've loved her since we were in high school."

"You're lucky to have her. If she wasn't already

married, I might abandon my celibacy and go after her. Think she'd go for a washed-up SEAL like me?"

"Don't go there. She's all mine." Hank stood, stretched and clapped a hand on Decker's back. "If I wasn't so tired—"

"—and if you didn't have such a beautiful bed partner," Decker interjected.

Hank nodded. "—I'd stay and see you home."

"I'm a big boy. I can get there on my own. I haven't had that much to drink, besides, I'm walking."

Hank glanced at Roxi. "Don't let him overindulge."

She gave him a mock salute and set Decker's drink on the bar in front of him. "I'll keep an eye on him." She followed with a wink at Decker that hit him straight in the gut.

Decker inhaled the scent of Roxi's perfume, tempted to lean over the counter for a bigger whiff. Instead, he stood and faced his friend, clasping his hand. "I don't know what I would have done if you hadn't been there for me after the accident."

Hank tugged on Decker's hand, pulling him into a bear hug. "I didn't do anything you wouldn't have done had the roles been reversed."

Decker clapped him hard on the back before releasing him. "Thanks for coming all the way out here when you didn't have to."

"Promise me you'll think about what I said." Hank threw some bills on the counter. "You deserve to be happy."

"I'll think about it," he lied. Thinking about moving on was harder than wallowing in grief. It meant letting go, and he wasn't sure he was ready to let go.

"Are you going back to your house?" Hank asked.

Decker shook his head. "I think I'll stay and finish my drink, since I'm not driving."

"Take care, man." Hank left the bar.

Once his friend disappeared through the door, Decker resumed his seat at the bar and downed the scotch in one long swallow.

"Hey. Slow down there." Roxi wiped her way across the bar toward him and sopped up the ring of condensation before he set down his glass. "You're supposed to sip and savor the flavor."

Decker stared down at the chunks of ice. "Don't judge. I'm supposed to be celebrating."

"Oh?" Roxi's brows rose. "What are you celebrating? Maybe I'll join you." She ditched the rag under the counter and filled a glass with Miller Lite from the tap.

He laughed, the sound more of a snort. "Today is my Alive Day."

She swallowed a healthy swig of her beer, her pretty, light brown brows wrinkling before she asked, "What's an Alive Day?" Roxi ran a hand through her thick hair lifting it off the back of her neck.

The scent of her shampoo wafted toward Decker and he inhaled, his eyes drifting closed. "Nothing. Never mind." Forcing himself to open his eyes and remain unfazed, he held out his empty glass. "Hit me, again."

She reached for the scotch and poured the liquid over the ice, the movements emphasizing the tautness of the muscles in her arms and the firmness of her breasts. For a brief moment, Decker considered Hank's words and almost asked Roxi if she wanted to have coffee with him sometime. He opened his mouth and closed it again.

Roxi set the bottle of scotch on the counter and raised her glass of beer.

Decker raised his scotch.

"Here's to being alive. For the most part, it beats the hell out of the alternative." Her voice was soft, sincere and hit Decker hard in the chest, pushing the air from his lungs.

His hand shook, and he set the glass down so hard, the liquid sloshed over on his hand. "I have to go."

Roxi set her glass aside, a frown marring her smooth forehead. "I'm sorry. Did I say something wrong?"

"No, you said the right thing." He forced a fake

smile and stood. "I just remembered I left my car running." He fumbled in his wallet for a couple bills.

For a long moment, Roxi stared at him, her lips firming.

When he held out the money, she pushed it back at him. "It's on the house."

"I insist." With his heart racing and the need to get out in the open almost a physical pain, he gripped her wrist and slapped the bills into her hand, ignoring the rush of electricity firing his nerves from where he touched her.

Roxi called to the town homeless man in the corner. "Saul, this is for you." She slapped the bills on the bar as Decker turned to leave. "If you need someone to talk to about leaving your car running, I'm a good listener."

Decker choked out, "I don't need anyone."

CHAPTER 2

ROXI WATCHED as Decker left the bar without looking back, practically running for the door. He had been coming to the bar all summer, living only a half mile down the beach in a quaint little bungalow with a wide, covered porch overlooking the ocean. She'd seen him sitting and standing on the decking, staring out at the sea at all hours of the day and night, as if searching for something. Maybe himself.

He kept his rich, dark hair trimmed neatly and, from what Roxi could tell, Decker appeared to be a man who had it all together. Until she stared into those deep green eyes, shadowed with pain. Except for this night when he'd shown up with another man, equally muscular and handsome, Decker usually sat alone and drank one scotch on the rocks, sometimes ordering food from the grill.

Women tried to talk to him, only to be ignored or politely turned away.

Roxi couldn't blame the women for hitting on him—the guy was incredibly good looking. But it was the haunted look in his green eyes that had touched something familiar inside. He'd experienced pain, something she could relate to. It drew her to him like metal to a magnet. All summer long, she'd fought the urge to be one of the women who tried to get him to notice her. He probably had enough of his own problems. He didn't need a woman with the kind of baggage she carried. Still, he was the only man for whom she'd even remotely considered letting down her guard.

Roxi shrugged and went back to work cleaning the bar and restocking the coolers for the next day. The regular crowd had thinned until the last customers left, promising to see her next summer.

"I've got this. Otis will be ready for his walk." Frank Hamner, her grill cook took the bag of trash she'd gathered. "You look like you could use the walk yourself."

She chuckled. "That bad?" Roxi touched a hand to her hair.

"You'll always be as pretty as the day your mom and dad brought you home from the hospital. But tonight, you have that faraway look you get when you sink back into bad places."

"I'm not sinking into bad places." She patted the

cook's face, her heart filled with love for the man who'd become the father she'd lost.

Frank covered her hand with his. "I wish I had been there for you. If I'd known you and your mom were in trouble..."

Roxi shook her head. "Mom was too proud to ask for help. And no one could have guessed something like that could happen."

"I wish she had asked for help. For your sake." The old retired drill sergeant, with the stern face and flat top hair cut might scare other people, but Roxi knew him for the kind and gentle soul who'd come along when she and her mother hit rock bottom. He'd brought them out to Cape Cod where he'd retired, and given Roxi a second chance at a life she never would have had in the dirty, dangerous streets of the Bronx where some mothers sold their children to feed their drug habit.

"What we can't change, we learn from," Roxi whispered her mother's mantra.

Frank snorted. "What I'm afraid is that you didn't learn the right things."

Roxi pushed her shoulders back. "I've learned how to take care of myself."

"Physically, but what about what's here?" He tapped his hand to his chest.

She smiled at Frank. "I would have thought you of all people would think emotion makes a person too weak to fight."

Frank shook his head. "Love gives a person a *reason* to fight—love for your family, your brothers in arms, hell, even your dog—without it, you have nothing."

"You're right. I love my family." She kissed the old man's grizzly face. "You. And I love Otis. I don't need anyone else."

"You're wrong."

"Says a man who lives alone." Roxi set a chair upside down on a table and reached for another. "Have you ever been in love?"

"Yes," Frank's voice said quietly.

Roxi turned and stared at the man who'd been her father's closest friend in the army. "Frank, were you married?"

He shook his head. "No, but I was in love."

Roxi had a hard time picturing the gruff, army sergeant in love. But then he loved her and even had affection for Otis. "With whom?"

He hiked the bag of trash up off the floor. "It doesn't matter now. She didn't feel the same way about me."

"Unrequited love." Roxi snorted. "All the more reason to steer clear of that kind of love."

"It's hard to do when your heart won't let go."

"But she didn't love you." Roxi set another chair upside down on the table.

A shadow passed over Frank's face. "I didn't love her any less because of it."

"So, you wasted your life mooning over her and what did it buy you?"

He stared at her for a long moment. "You."

When the one word sank in, Roxi's heart squeezed so tightly, her eyes stung. "You loved my mother?"

He nodded. "But she loved your father—my friend."

Roxi shook her head, the tears welling. "Oh, Frank…"

"Now don't go getting misty-eyed over this old coot. I knew the stakes, and I knew how much your mother loved your father and he loved her. I only wanted her to be happy." He turned with the big bag of trash. "Enough about me. You need to get on with your life. Don't waste it working yourself to death in this bar." He turned back and gave her one of his sternest looks. "And don't think you're not worthy of love because of what happened. You have a lot to offer. Don't sell yourself short."

Still stunned by Frank's revelation, she gave him a watery smile and popped a salute that would have made her father proud. "Yes, sir."

His frown deepened. "And don't call me sir. I work for a living." Frank exited through the back door, carrying the bag.

With a lot on her mind, Roxi trudged up the steps to her apartment over the bar where she was greeted by a wiggling, happy Otis, the one hundred twenty-pound German shepherd Frank had given her when she'd moved out on her own, taking up residence over the bar. He'd been trained by one of Frank's old Army buddies who'd been a dog handler in the military police.

Otis waited patiently while she snapped on his leash and picked up her heavy flashlight, the one she carried for protection, more than for illuminating her way. She rarely used it unless the night was cloudy. Roxi never felt in danger as long as Otis was around. Without him, she probably wouldn't step outside in the dark.

Fortunately, the moon shone brightly. Roxi could see as clearly as if it were the middle of the day.

She set out along the sand, unclipping Otis's leash as soon as she passed the pier. Otis shot ahead, chasing waves along the shoreline. He loved the water and the beach as much as Roxi. He circled back behind her and chased a crab that ultimately buried itself in the wet sand. Not to be deterred, Otis dug into the sand, spewing it out behind him.

Roxi laughed and kept walking.

A figure detached itself from the stilts of a beach house ahead and walked across the sand to the edge of the water.

By size and the breadth of his shoulders, Roxi guessed the figure to be a man, and not just any man, but the one who'd been on her mind more and more with each passing day—John Decker.

Her heartbeat skittered against her ribs and she slowed to a stop, her bare toes curling in the wet sand.

Decker's face remained turned toward the sea and he wore nothing but a pair of shorts or swim trunks. Moonlight glimmered off his naked chest, turning it a silvery blue. As he walked toward the water his pace increased until he ran into the surf lapping against the shore.

What was he doing? The tide report indicated the water wasn't safe with the coming storm churning the sea.

Decker struck out, swimming hard out to sea. His arms sliced through the water, powering him farther away from shore, closer and closer to the area known for its wicked riptide.

"Decker!" Roxi ran toward the point at which he'd entered the water and waved. "Decker! Come back!"

Either he was ignoring her shouts or he couldn't hear them with his head in the water, because he continued on his race toward a potentially deadly situation.

"Decker!" Roxi glanced to the right and left. The lifeguard towers were on the other side of the pier, too far to go for a life preserver.

Decker was too far out to hear her voice. If she

could get close enough to warn him he might have a chance to turn around before he got sucked out even further by a riptide. Roxi waded into the water, her pulse pounding her stomach knotted. She was a good swimmer, having lived the last fourteen years on the Cape. She knew how to ride the tide into shore, but even she wasn't naive enough to swim in riptide situations.

Cupping her hands around her mouth, Roxi shouted again.

Decker's arms slowed and he glided to a stop.

Roxi gathered another breath.

The dark head, now only a speck on the ocean, disappeared.

"Decker?" she whispered, her heart lodged in her throat. Then she dove into the water and swam as hard as she'd ever swum toward the spot she'd last seen him. She pushed back all of the warnings Frank and her mother had drilled into her head as she rose on the swell of a small wave and scanned ahead.

There. A hundred yards ahead, she spied Decker's dark head, drifting south, carried by the current.

Otis barked from the shoreline, the sound carrying out to where Roxi paused to breathe, her lungs burning with the need for oxygen. She drew in a deep breath and yelled, "Decker!" A wave slapped her in the face, and she sucked salt water into her lungs.

For a moment she sputtered, coughing and fighting to keep her head above the water as she cleared her lungs. When she could breathe again, she searched for Decker's dark head on the water's surface.

The swells had increased, and she couldn't see him. Treading water, she turned toward the shore where Otis danced along the water's edge, barking furiously. Once again, she turned toward the open sea, but couldn't find Decker. The tide was pulling her south, past the pier. If she didn't start angling toward the shore, she might not make it back. Now the fight to find Decker became a struggle to save herself. If she could get to shore, she would send out a rescue boat to find Decker, which she should have done in the first place.

Forcing herself to remain calm she struck out toward shore, swimming with the current while cutting at a diagonal toward the shore. The tide pulled at her like hands gripping her legs, dragging her toward the open sea. She fought against its clutches, kicking as hard as she could to break away. It seemed that for every inch forward, she lost two, hauling her backward.

Her arms ached and the muscles in her legs burned. Roxi slowed and treaded water long enough to rest and catch her breath.

A figure surfaced beside her, startling her, but she was too tired to scream.

When she realized it was Decker, she almost cried in relief. Moonlight glistened off his wet hair, making it appear blue-black. His powerful shoulders rose above the surface as they bobbed with each swell.

"Don't give up." Decker grabbed her hand and pulled her against him with one arm, his free one stroking the water to keep them both afloat.

"I'm okay," she insisted, not feeling okay, but unwilling to let him take on the burden of her, when she shouldn't have swum after him in the first place. What had she been thinking? "I'm just resting before I swim again."

"Let me know when you're ready." A wave splashed over them before he could continue. "We'll make it to shore together."

She nodded, the salty tang of water on her lips, a surge of hope fueling her tired muscles. Roxi kicked hard headed toward the sandy beach.

Decker paced her, silently swimming at her side, occasionally reaching out to pull her along.

Slowly, they edged toward land, and finally, Roxi's toes encountered sand. She laughed as she staggered to her feet and slogged through knee-deep water toward a frantic Otis.

A strong arm slipped around her waist adding strength to her flagging reserves.

When they reached dry land, Roxi dropped to

her knees on the gritty sand and rolled onto her back, completely drained of energy.

Otis licked her face, whining and shaking all over.

"Are you okay?" Decker knelt and leaned over her, peering into her face.

She forced her lips to curve upward. "I will be."

"Good." His brows dipped into a V and moonlight reflected off his eyes. "Then why the hell were you swimming alone this late at night?"

CHAPTER 3

DECKER COULDN'T STOP the surge of anger radiating through his body. Yeah, he didn't know what he'd been thinking, swimming at midnight when riptide warnings had been all over the radio earlier that day, and the colored flag had been flown on the lifeguard stands. But he couldn't sit around his beach cottage, wide awake, guilt-ridden, lusting after a woman on the anniversary of his wife's death. He'd walked out onto his deck wanting to shout to the heavens *Why didn't I die?* No matter how many times he reiterated those words, he still had no answer. With so much pent up frustration and energy locked inside, he'd walked down the steps, his chest pinched, his throat tight.

He'd kept walking until his feet hit the wet sand. Then he ran, splashing through the waves, and dove into the ocean. Swimming hard, his arms pounded the water, his feet churned behind him. In the back of his mind, he must have thought the salt water and waves were the only thing that could wash the old memories from his head. If he swam faster, he didn't have time to think about the image of his wife's dead body lying on the side of the road, that maybe it would fade, and he could move on with living his empty life. Yes, Allison's image faded.

And yet, no matter how hard he pushed himself, Roxi's curvy body and smiling face never left his consciousness. Her silky, blond hair a man could wrap his fingers in, those perky breasts barely encased in that impossible tank top, and the rounded curve of her bottom twitching side to side in the frayed denim cutoffs, played over and over in his mind like a continuous rerun of a movie.

When his lungs burned for oxygen and his arms and legs couldn't take it anymore, he'd slowed to a stop and treaded water. By that time, he'd been far from shore, the water as choppy and seeming to be as disturbed as he was. Then he'd heard the distant rapid-fire barking of a dog. He'd squinted, trying to make out the animal in the bright moonlight. It appeared to be a German shepherd. The only German shepherd he knew along this stretch of the beach belonged to the pretty blond bar owner so firmly rooted in his head. Decker searched for what had upset the dog only to see someone swimming toward him.

Some of the dog's panic seeped into Decker's gut, and he'd started toward the head bobbing just above the surface, arms cleaving the water in steady strokes, propelling him toward her.

He'd been stunned to realize Roxi was out swimming. He'd started back to shore on a course to intercept the woman, only to find the current was working against him. No matter how hard he swam he wasn't getting any closer to the shore, but Roxi was getting closer to him.

The sea grew choppier and he only caught brief glimpses of her, recognizing when she'd come to the realization that she was in trouble. Roxi turned and swam with the current, angling toward the shore, her strokes slowing the longer she swam. When she'd stopped, Decker finally caught up to her.

Having used up most of his strength to chase his memories away, he feared he wouldn't have any left to help her to shore. But the bar owner was tougher than he'd assumed. With only a little help and encouragement, she'd swum with him all the way back to terra firma.

Now that they were safely on shore, he couldn't hold back the rush of relief and the release of fear that she might not have made it back. It all bubbled up with the anger he'd had with himself, and he let it loose on her. "Why were you swimming when you knew damn well there was a riptide?"

She stared up at him, her eyes rounding, a film of tears glazing them, reflecting the moon shining down on her wet skin. A shuddering sob rose from her throat. She raised a hand to her mouth, but her shoulders shook. The sob turned into a giggle, the giggle into laughter, catching on yet another sob. "I thought I could save you." Tears slipped from the corners of her eyes as she shook her head and reached to touch his arm. "Instead, you saved me."

Decker frowned. "Save me? From what?"

She sniffed and brushed the salty water and tears from her cheeks. "The riptide."

When her words sank in, his gut clenched. "You weren't out swimming for fun?"

Roxi shook her head. "No. I saw you go in. When you didn't stop swimming out, I shouted... several times. I couldn't let you keep going."

"What were you going to do had you caught up to me?"

Draping an arm across her eyes, she lay still in the sand. "I hadn't thought that far ahead."

He raked a hand through his wet hair. "Are you always this impulsive?"

"Never."

"Damn, Roxi," he said. "Didn't anyone teach you that riptides are dangerous?"

She dropped her arm to her side, her brows

furrowing. "I know about riptides. I've lived on this island a lot longer than you."

"Yet you swam out to save a man who is almost twice your size in an area with notoriously dangerous currents." Decker's lips thinned into a straight line. "Unbelievable."

"I didn't plan on getting caught in the tide. I didn't plan anything. I just couldn't let you...I couldn't stand by and do nothing, when you..." She closed her eyes and draped her arm over them again. "Whatever. Go away. I don't need you telling me what to do." Then under her breath she muttered, "It never fails. No good deed goes unpunished."

Roxi lay against the wet sand, her hair a tangled mess, her heaving chest slowly relaxing into steady breathing.

Sitting beside her, Decker stared at the brave, stupid, incredibly beautiful woman whose wet tank top emphasized the pucker of her nipples beneath her white lacy bra. She was the reason he'd gone into the ocean in the first place. Her perky, happy, no-nonsense work at the bar had captured his attention the first time he'd entered and hadn't let go for the entire summer he'd been at the Cape.

Now, lying in the moonlight, her hair a mess, her body covered in sticky salt water and clumps of sand, she'd never been more beautiful.

His groin tightened, and he fought the urge to

touch her, to feel how soft her skin was when he wasn't trying to save her from drowning in a riptide.

Her eyes blinked open. "Why are you still here?"

"I didn't want to leave you alone."

"I'm not alone." She turned her head to the dog lying in the sand beside her. "I have Otis."

A smile pulled at Decker's lips. "You do have Otis. If it wasn't for him, I wouldn't have known you were out there." He reached across her body to ruffle the dog's head.

Roxi's brows furrowed. "Hey, Otis. You're supposed to protect me from the enemy, not join the other side."

"Oh, so now I'm the enemy?" Decker chuckled, and the sound faded at the thought that she considered him the enemy. "Why am I the enemy?"

"All men are the enemy," she said, her voice little more than a sigh. "Especially the ones who want to take advantage of a girl walking by herself."

Her words jolted his gut. "And I'm taking advantage of you?"

Her lips twisted. "You're hovering over me like a vulture looking for his next meal."

"Sorry, didn't mean to hover." He flopped down on his back in the sand and stared up at the sky.

Otis rose up on all fours and walked around Roxi to lie down beside Decker.

Roxi snorted. "Traitor."

Decker raised tired arms. "I had nothing to do with it. Dogs like me. So, sue me." He dropped a hand onto Otis's fur and rubbed him. "Is he always this friendly?"

"Not with men."

He angled his head to stare at her. "Have you got something against men?"

"No," she said, a little too quickly, and rolled onto her side to face him. "You know why *I* swam out in a riptide, but you didn't tell me why *you* did."

"No, I didn't." Decker stared up at the sky, the full moon shining brightly down on them, wrapping them in a surreal world where nothing else existed but the sand, the ocean, and the two people lying on the beach. Oh, and the dog panting in his face.

"Well?" Roxi pushed up on one elbow.

"Well what?" Decker didn't face her but could see the intent expression on her face in his peripheral vision.

"You looked like a shark was after you, and like you had every intention of swimming all the way to France to get away from it."

He shrugged, the gritty sand rubbing against his skin. "Maybe a shark *was* after me."

"Did it have anything to do with celebrating your Alive Day?" she asked softly. For a long moment she stared down at him. When he didn't answer, she dropped to her back and faced the moon. "You don't have to answer. Some things don't bear remembering."

Her words hit home, and his chest swelled with all the emotion he'd tried to swim out of his system but hadn't quite managed to do. Now, too tired to fight it, he let it wash over him, filling every cell in his body. "I should have died that day."

"But you didn't."

"No. But my wife did." There, he said it. He told her something he didn't share with anyone who hadn't known him at the time of the accident.

"Sucks, doesn't it?" Roxi said, her voice soft.

His eyes stung, and a knot formed in his throat. He hadn't shed a tear over his loss, feeling numb more than anything else. Afraid if he let his emotions take over, he'd lose control and never find his way back.

"Sometimes dying seems the easier way out," she said, her tone stronger. "Then you don't have to feel the pain over and over again."

"Yeah." Decker turned toward Roxi, realizing she wasn't talking about his pain. Her gaze fixed on the moon as if seeing into the past, not the bright round orb hanging in the sky.

"What's your story?" he asked. "Who did you lose?"

She snorted. "It doesn't matter. What's past is past. We have to continue breathing until we take our last breath, don't we?" Roxi pushed to a sitting position. "Well, thanks for helping me back to shore."

Decker rolled to his feet before she did and extended his hand.

She stared at it and shook her head. "Thanks, but I don't need anyone."

Decker frowned. She hadn't said she didn't need *help,* she'd said she didn't need *anyone.* "We all need a hand once in a while. Take it. Your legs will be like jelly after that swim. Mine are."

"I'm tougher than I look." She pushed to her feet, staggered and would have fallen if Decker hadn't reached out and pulled her against him.

Her soft curves fit against his hard planes, reminding him of what he'd been missing in his life.

God, he'd loved Allison. She'd been beautiful with her short cap of rich brown hair, and dark brown eyes. At five feet five inches, her body was slim, almost too thin and her big eyes had always reminded him of a homeless puppy who needed to be protected, cared for and loved unconditionally. He'd failed her by not keeping her safe from harm. Allison had been one of the kindest, gentlest souls he'd ever met. He hadn't deserved her, and he'd lost her.

Now he stared down at the curvy woman in his arms, shorter than Allison, but more solidly built, her muscles toned from exercise and hard work, her skin lightly tanned and eyes such a bright blue they rivaled the shine of the moon. Her lips were full and lush, and all he could think about in that moment was kissing them.

His head lowered.

Roxi's eyelids drooped and her stiff body melted into his, her gaze shifting lower. Before he could kiss her, she leaned up on her toes and pressed her lips to his in a brief kiss.

Decker's arms tightened around her and he deepened the kiss.

Her hands slid up his chest and locked around the back of his neck, tugging him closer.

He swept his tongue across her salty lips. When she let out a soft gasp, he plunged past her teeth to sweep the length of her tongue in a ravenous caress. He couldn't get enough. His groin tightened, and his erection pressed into her belly.

Roxi's body stiffened in an instant, and she went from warm and pliant in his arms to shoving against his chest, pushing hard enough he let go and staggered backward, still holding her to keep his balance.

"Let go of me," she whispered.

"Okay." When he was steady on his feet, he released her.

She stepped out of reach, wobbled and then sat hard in the sand.

"What's wrong?" he squatted on his haunches in front of her. "Did I hurt you?"

"No." She brushed strands of hair out of her eyes. "Just leave me alone."

He shook his head. "Not until I see you home safely."

"I can make it on my own, thank you."

"I know. But after nearly causing you to drown, I feel responsible for you."

"Well, don't." She stood, swaying slightly. "I have Otis."

Decker brushed his hand over the dog's fur. "Yes, you do. But I'm not taking no for an answer."

"Suit yourself. But don't kiss me." Roxi pressed the back of her hand over her mouth, her eyes still wide, almost scared.

Had he done that to her? "You kissed me first."

Her hand fell to her side. "It won't happen again." She spun toward the bar. "Come, Otis."

Roxi walked away, her footsteps steadier with each step.

How she did it, Decker didn't know. His legs were like jelly and exhaustion tugged at every muscle in his body. Had she not come after him when she did, had Otis not been with Roxi, barking so loudly, Decker might be floating out to sea, too far out to swim back and too tired to fight the current. Hell, had Roxi not shown up, he might not have cared enough to make it back to shore. In more ways than one, Roxi had saved his life.

When they arrived at the bar, Roxi didn't stop until she reached the rear staircase. With her foot braced on the bottom riser, she faced him. "Thanks for saving me."

Decker shook his head, amazed that this woman thought he'd saved her. "I should be thanking you. If you hadn't swum after me..." He shook his head and gave her half a smile. "I might be halfway to France by now or eaten by sharks." He took her hand in his. "Thank you." With his gaze on hers, he lifted her hand and raised it halfway to his lips, daring her to yank it back.

She didn't, allowing him to sweep his mouth across her knuckles. Her fingers tightened around his. "Decker."

"Yes, Roxi?"

"Sometimes living is harder than dying."

He nodded, his fingers squeezing hers.

"But I'm glad you didn't die." She pulled her hand loose and ran up the stairs.

Otis stood at Decker's side, his ears perked.

At the top landing, Roxi yanked open her door and held it wide. "Come on, Traitor."

Otis glanced up at Decker.

"Go on," Decker waved his hand.

"Really?" Roxi shook her head. "I'm getting a new dog."

Otis climbed the stairs and entered the house like he was the owner, not Roxi.

With one last glance at Decker, Roxi entered and closed the door behind her.

Decker whispered, "Happy Alive Day."

CHAPTER 4

Once Roxi closed the door, she leaned her back against it and slid to the floor, her knees weak, her body shaking and not from almost being lost out to sea. She shook because of a little kiss that should never have happened. Why had she stood on her toes and initiated it? *Why*?

She trembled, and her blood ran hot, running through her veins like smoldering, molten lava, warming her cold body from tip to toe. Normally, she pushed away from men out of fear of their superior strength. This time, she'd pushed away out of fear of her own core heating, of her own breath-catching, gut-wrenching, raging desire. Never had she felt anything like what she'd felt when her breasts smashed against Decker's chest, forcing the wind from her lungs. Her control had slipped, and she'd sunk into him, tingling all over. His gaze had captured hers and Decker had lowered his head. At that moment, Roxi had wanted to kiss him so badly she'd met him halfway, pressing her lips to his.

When he'd cinched her closer...Oh, Lord!

Roxi wrapped her arms around her middle and rocked forward, a moan rising up her throat. She couldn't get close enough. The longing swept over her, crushing her in its grip. How could she long for someone when she was afraid to be intimate with a man? Afraid he'd learn the truth about her.

Otis dropped to the floor beside her and laid a paw across her lap and his chin on the paw. He gazed up into her eyes as if seeing into her soul.

"Oh, Otis. What am I supposed to do?" She stroked his fur, tears welling in her eyes. "I can't be with a man. Didn't tonight prove it?"

The dog whined softly and nudged her hand, encouraging her to keep stroking him.

As she did, calm spread through her and exhaustion pulled at her eyelids. If she didn't get up and shower, she'd fall asleep where she sat. Her problems wouldn't solve themselves by dozing off on a hardwood floor and waking with a sore back. She had a business to run. Work would keep her focused and give her no time to wish for something she'd never have.

She forced herself to go through the motions of showering and dressing for bed. The sun would be up all too soon, and the supply truck would be there before noon. Reminding herself to worry only about the things she could control, Roxi crawled into bed and closed her eyes. Immediately, images filled her mind of Decker and his incredible physique leaning over her. His body shimmering as the moonlight refracted off the droplets of water covering his chest.

If only she could relax around the man and be like any normal, red-blooded woman, she might have a stab at a real life.

Then again, Decker was still grieving over his dead wife. Even if Roxi could work past the lingering trauma of being brutalized at the innocent age of thirteen, she still couldn't compete with a dead woman. One who'd had Decker's love and complete commitment.

Roxi sighed and turned on her side, pulling a pillow close to her body. For the first time since she was thirteen, she wanted to be held in a man's arms. The pillow she snuggled with wasn't nearly as satisfying as being close to Decker's body, her skin touching his. What would it be like to lie in a bed with the man? To let him touch her? To make love?

Her belly clenched, and she closed her eyes.

Would she tense and panic like she did anytime a man got close? Hell, he'd only kissed her and she'd pushed him away. Then she'd told him not to kiss her. Even if she wanted a second chance with

Decker, he was the type of man who'd respect her wishes.

Roxi tossed and turned, twisting in her sheets until she finally fell into a troubled sleep where a strange man held her down and tried to rape her. It was the same nightmare she'd lived with off and on for over a decade. Only this time a good man with dark hair and deep green eyes swam ashore and rescued her before the bad guy brutalized her. The good guy held her in his arms, whispering reassuring words of love. Then he kissed her, and her body burned with desire.

She stripped him of his shorts and licked the salty sea water off his skin, memorizing every inch of his body before she came down over him, taking him inside where no man had gone since she was thirteen.

On her knees, she rode him until her body tensed, and her insides erupted in a beautiful explosion. When at last she lay down beside him, he gathered her into his arms and held her, his arms loose about her, giving her the freedom to choose whether to stay or go.

She stayed.

This was what sex was supposed to be. Two souls making a connection on more than just a physical level.

Roxi opened her eyes and stared at the luminous green lights of her alarm clock and groaned.

Her body was covered in a thin layer of perspiration and she ached low in her belly, her center warm and wet from the insanely erotic dream.

Unbeknownst to him, John Decker had found a way beneath her tough shell and refused to release her to go back behind the wall she'd built around her heart.

Lying awake well into the early hours of the morning, Roxi struggled to eradicate the man from her thoughts so that she might sleep. Despite all of her attempts, she couldn't shake the image of his naked, wet chest as he leaned over her, the moonlight reflecting off his inky black hair.

Damn. What if he showed up at the bar that night? How would she act?

Her insides warmed. Her core tightened, and her lips tingled.

Decker posed a danger to the thin thread she held over the control she'd fought so long to maintain. She had to get over those feelings before she saw him again.

"**Hey Decker**!"

The voice jerked him awake and made him blink at the gray daylight, hitting him square in the face. Decker glanced around, at first disoriented until he remembered trudging along the beach at zero-dark-thirty in the morning and collapsing in an Adirondack chair on his deck without attempting to make it to his shower and bed. He didn't want to be confined to a space after all that had happened with Roxi. And he sure as hell didn't want to go to bed and wish she was lying beside him.

On the anniversary of his wife's death, he didn't want to lie awake in his empty bed when he'd had the pleasure of kissing a beautiful woman.

"Yo, dude. Are you all right?" Hank climbed the steps to the stilted deck and leaned against the railing.

Decker pushed a hand through his hair, sticky and stiff from the salt water that had dried there. "What time is it?" he asked, his voice gravelly with sleep.

"Nearly ten." Hank glanced around. "I take it you slept here last night?"

Pushing himself out of the chair, Decker stretched sore muscles. "Yeah."

His friend gave him a hard stare. "How much did you drink last night?"

Decker glared at his friend. "I wasn't drunk."

"Yeah, and we all like to sleep outside on the deck." Hank shook his head. "You going to be all right?"

Rather than give Hank his canned answer, Decker thought for a moment before he nodded. "Yeah. I am." And, oddly, it was true.

"You're not going to mope around the Cape all winter, are you? Because if I find out that's what you're doing, I'll have to come back out here. And you know how I hate coming to the Cape when it's cold and rainy, or worse, covered two feet deep in snow."

Decker raised his hands. "I promise not to mope. I have work to do, and I'm okay with cold, rainy and snow-covered ground."

"Do yourself a favor and get to know the locals. They're a hardy lot, and they'll have your back if you should run into any trouble."

One particular local came to mind, and his pulse kicked up a notch. "I'll do that." And maybe he would. If she didn't shut him out like she had the previous night, after sharing an unforgettable kiss.

Hank stuck out a hand. "It was good to see you again, Decker."

Decker gripped the man's hand and pulled him into a quick hug. "Thanks for being there for me last night."

"That's what friends are for." Hank turned and walked toward the steps. "Don't be a stranger. If you get too cold and wet, head to Montana. I'll put you to work with my Brotherhood Protectors."

"I'm not ready to be anyone's bodyguard."

"We have other missions."

"I'm not ready," Deck insisted.

"Well then, you can stay at the ranch with Sadie and me, until you figure out what you're ready for."

"Don't you need to check with Sadie before inviting people into your home?"

"Sadie knows your story, and she was the one to make the offer. She's waiting in the car, if you want to verify."

"That's okay. I'm not really dressed for company."

"She wouldn't care."

Decker clapped a hand on Hank's back. "She's a keeper. Don't screw it up."

"Not a chance. I got lucky when I found her." Hank raised a hand. "Take care. I expect to see you before the holidays. Don't be a stranger."

Decker rounded the side of the house and stood on the front deck.

Sadie leaned out the window of Hank's SUV. "Come for Christmas!" she shouted. "We have plenty of room at the ranch."

"I'll think about it," Decker responded and waved.

Hank climbed into his car and drove away, along with half the inhabitants of the Cape in the usual mass exodus after the last day of summer vacation for most people. In a few short days, the Cape would be a veritable ghost town with summer cottages closed for the long, cold winter. The water sport rentals and the shaved ice stand were buttoned up, supplies stored until the next summer when school was out and a new wave of people moved in.

A steady stream of vehicles lined the road, driving slowly out of town.

Facing his first winter on the Cape, Decker hadn't been sure about his decision. Up until last night, he'd left open the option to move back to Montana at the end of the summer season.

He'd moved to the Cape to leave behind the home his wife had decorated. In Norfolk, a city full of people, he'd felt more alone than ever. He'd hoped that a change of scenery might shake him out of the hole he'd crawled into after Allison's death.

Selling their house in Virginia had been the first step. When Hank had told him about a cottage on Cape Cod that was for sale close to his vacation cottage, it gave him the perfect location to start over in a completely different environment. He had some money saved up that he could live on for a while until he decided what kind of work he wanted to get into full time. On more than one occasion, Hank had offered him a job with his personal security agency the Brotherhood Protectors back in his home state of Montana. He hadn't given him an answer yet. He wanted the time on his own at the Cape to get his head on straight.

The summer had flown by with his working odd jobs, mostly in construction and maintenance, physically demanding jobs requiring his full concentration. At night, he worked at his computer, performing cyber security work, reviewing websites and social media for potential terrorist threats. It didn't pay much, and it wasn't as exciting as being a Navy SEAL on a mission, but he felt he was still doing something toward keeping his country safe.

The cottage on the beach had provided the perfect balm to his soul, allowing him a place to go at the end of the day, without any of his family and friends stopping in to ask how he was. With the exception of Hank and Sadie who'd spent the past week at the Cape.

After Allison's death, Decker had left the Navy and drifted from job to job, not sure what he wanted or where he was going next. The sale of his house in Norfolk gave him the money he needed to buy the cottage on Cape Cod so he wasn't strapped for cash. He had time to find his way and decide what he wanted to do with the rest of his life. The odd job of cyber-sleuthing for the government helped to keep money in his coffers.

Once all the tourists were gone, Decker would have the beach very much to himself. No more kids throwing Frisbees onto his deck. The only people he'd see were the locals. Like Roxi walking Otis, maybe stopping long enough to ask how he was doing. If she wasn't so scared of him, he'd invite her up on his deck for a beer. They'd sit outside and watch the sunset, talking about the different colors spreading across the sky.

Decker reminded himself she'd never stopped by his place, and probably wouldn't. After his dip in the sea during a strong riptide, she might think he was a nut job and stay as far away from him as she could.

But that kiss had not been one-sided.

Damn it. Why couldn't he get her out of his mind?

He entered the cottage, grabbed his laptop and went to work searching the internet, not stopping until his stomach growled so much he was forced to seek sustenance. A glance at the clock on his desktop indicated it was near noon. Though he already knew the contents of his empty fridge, he checked anyway, hoping to find a slice of leftover pizza or a jar of jelly. He had peanut butter, but a quick check in the breadbox proved he was out of bread. If he wanted to eat, he had to go to the grocery store or eat at a restaurant.

Decker showered, dressed in shorts and a polo shirt, and slipped into a pair of tennis shoes. Grabbing his keys, he headed out in search of food. The slight breeze of the morning had picked up, lifting discarded burger wrappers and plastic grocery bags, carrying them along the sandy shoreline.

Little puffs of clouds skittered across the sky as if in a hurry to escape the Cape.

The restlessness in the air permeated Decker's senses. He passed his car with only a brief glance and chose instead to walk down the beach. Despite his vow to stay as far away from Roxi Lanier as possible, Decker found himself at the entrance to the Gone Fishin' Bar & Grill. It was the closest place to his cottage to get lunch, and the food was good. So what if Roxi worked there? He couldn't avoid her forever and, frankly, he didn't want to.

Roxi wasn't at the bar, mixing drinks and chatting with customers. For that matter, most of the summer crowd had left during the day, headed back to the cities, their summer fun over for the year. A few stragglers were scattered around the tables, finishing lunch and drinking beer. Soon, the temperatures would drop and rain and snow would claim the Cape. The summer and weekend revelers would be gone, and the locals would hunker down.

Frank, the crusty old cook came out of the kitchen, wiping his hands on a dishtowel.

"Is the grill still open?" Decker asked.

"It is," Frank said in his booming voice.

Decker glanced around.

"If you're looking for a waitress, the summer staff left today, Marcy called in sick and Roxi had to run to the store for supplies. She should be back any minute. What can I get you?"

"A burger with all the works, fried pickles and water."

Frank nodded toward the tables. "Seat yourself. I'll be back with your water when I get your burger on the grill."

Decker chose to sit at the bar. When Roxi returned, he'd apologize for kissing her and thank her for coming after him when he'd gone out too far into the ocean. He'd been foolish.

Frank returned with a beer mug full of ice water.

One of the groups of people rose from their seats, tossed several bills on the table and waved. "See ya next year!" they called out.

Frank nodded. "We'll be here."

The door closed behind the group leaving only Decker and the last foursome lingering over beer and cold French fries.

Frank swiped a rag over the counter.

"How long has Gone Fishin' been here?" Decker swirled the ice in his glass.

"I bought it fifteen years ago and sold it a year and a half ago."

Decker glanced up. "Sold it?"

"Yeah. Roxi owns it now. I just want to work until I can't, take off when I want and enjoy what's left of my life."

"You're not old enough to retire."

"I'm old." Frank laughed. "And I should be sick,

as much grease as I inhale back in the kitchen." He threw the dishtowel over his shoulder. "Speaking of grease, I'd better go check on that burger before I start a fire."

He hurried back to the kitchen and returned a few minutes later with the burger, fried pickles and condiments. "Can I get you anything else?"

"No, this looks perfect." His mouth watered at the scent of grilled burger. Decker loaded it with all the fixings and clapped the bun on top.

"Can I get you beer to go with that?"

"No." Decker held up a hand. "I had more than enough to drink last night."

"When are you heading out?" Frank asked.

"I'm not." Decker lifted the burger. "What about you? Will Roxi close the place over the winter?"

"No, she runs it all year round. Most stores and restaurants close during the winter. Not the Gone Fishin'. Since Roxi took over, she's upgraded the Bar & Grill to a *sports* Bar & Grill." Frank pointed to the corners, one by one. "She added the large televisions and keeps sports on at all times. This is now the place to be to watch football games and other sports or just to hang out with friends. Folks love it. And they love Roxi."

"She seems to have a lot going for her. I'm surprised she's not married with a couple of kids running around the place."

Frank shook his head, the smile fading from his

eyes. "I wish she was. I doubt she'll ever get married."

"Why not?"

Frank's eyes narrowed. "Why do you care?"

Decker shrugged. "I don't know. She's pretty and she always has a smile on her face." *Except when I kiss her.* "I'd have thought she'd be snapped up by some lucky guy."

For a long moment Frank stared at Decker—no, make that *glared* at Decker. "There are things you don't know about Roxi. Things you'll have to ask her yourself. She's had a hard enough life without some city dude screwing it up again. Don't mess with her, or I'll take you down." The old man's lip curled up on one side. "If *she* doesn't take you down first."

Decker didn't blink and didn't back down at Frank's warning. *You're not in the market for a relationship.* He repeated the mantra in his head. "I like Roxi. I wouldn't hurt her." *Not intentionally.*

"Good." Frank squared his shoulders. "I'll get a refill on your drink."

"I'll get it," a female voice said behind Decker. "What are you having?" Roxi entered the building and walked around him, carrying a reusable canvas bag filled with groceries. She smiled at Frank. "If you'll take these, I'll get this customer's drink."

Frank took the bag. "He had water." With a long

narrow-eyed glance at Decker, he left the bar and returned to the kitchen.

Roxi spun to face Decker, a smile on her face. Her smile froze, and her eyes rounded, a slow flush rose in her cheeks. "Oh. It's you."

CHAPTER 5

HEAT FILLED Roxi's cheeks and her lips tingled with the memory of Decker's kiss. "Water, was it?" She slid behind the bar, snatched his glass from the counter, and filled it with ice and water from the tap in quick, efficient movements. She set the glass on the counter and water sloshed over the side. "Sorry." She bent to retrieve a clean rag from a drawer and sopped up the moisture. When she stopped fussing, her hands shook so she shoved them behind her back and forced what she hoped was a carefree, I'm-not-at-all-attracted-to-you smile. "Is there anything else I can do for you?"

Decker nodded. "You can have dinner with me tonight."

She shook her head before he finished. "I'm working. Most of the staff left for the summer and my fulltime waitress is out sick."

"Then have coffee with me," he persisted.

Her heart skipped several beats and she almost agreed. "I can't."

"You have to walk Otis sometime. Let me walk with you."

On cue, Otis entered the bar, sat beside Decker's chair and nuzzled his leg.

Decker grinned. "I think you're outvoted." He scratched the dog behind the ears. "If it makes you feel better, I won't kiss you." His gaze rose to capture hers and he added softly, "If you don't kiss me first."

"I don't know." She bit down on her bottom lip again. Being with Decker stirred up feelings she wasn't sure she could handle.

"I want to thank you for saving my life." Decker stared at her, his face sincere, his gaze compelling. "Please."

For a long moment, she debated the foolishness of leading on a man who could never be more than a casual acquaintance. She took a deep breath and said, "I walk Otis around three—in between the lunch and evening crowd." Hell, she'd done it now. When she should have said no, she agreed to walk with him. Well, what could happen? She would be on a public beach in full daylight. With people around, she wouldn't be tempted to kiss him.

Her gaze shifted to his lips. Just because she was tempted to kiss him now, didn't mean she'd be tempted on the beach. They'd be moving, not staring at each other.

"Three o'clock, then," he said, smiling. "I'll be on the beach between the bar and the pier."

Roxi nodded. "Okay. Now if you don't need anything else, I have supplies to unload."

She hurried back out to her SUV, gathered several bags and carried them into the bar, passing Decker on the way to the kitchen where she unloaded groceries onto the counter.

Frank stood at the preparation counter, his gaze on the window between the bar and the kitchen, a frown pulling his bushy gray brows together. "If Decker is bothering you, just say the word and I'll send him on his way."

Bothering her? Oh, yeah, he bothered her all right. But not the way Frank was talking about. He made her feel things she wasn't sure she should be feeling. With her old friend glaring out the window at Decker, Roxi laughed. "He's not bothering me."

"Like I said. Say the word and I can show him the door and tell him he's not welcome to ever come back."

Roxi leaned up on her toes and kissed Frank's grizzled cheek. "Thanks, but I'm not thirteen anymore. I'll be twenty-seven next month, and I'm perfectly capable of taking care of myself."

"Doesn't hurt to have backup. Just in case."

"I know. And I appreciate the sentiment." She

hugged him briefly and went back to work putting the supplies on the shelves.

"What do you know about Decker?"

That he could kiss like nobody's business and his muscles were rock-solid. "Not a lot." Roxi's body heated.

"Keep Otis with you, when you're around him."

She nodded, hiding a smile. "I will." She didn't tell Frank that Otis seemed to be on Decker's side.

Frank reached around her to grab the sugar canister. "I worry about you."

"I know you do. You're worse than my mother was."

"You know your mother never forgave herself for what that man did to you when you lived in the city."

"How could she have anticipated something like that happening to me? I was thirteen. I thought I knew everything. I broke her one major rule and stepped out of the apartment for what I thought would be five minutes to run to the store."

She'd wanted to surprise her mother by having dinner ready for her. The woman worked two jobs and rarely got home before eight at night. Roxi wanted to make the only thing she knew how—spaghetti. Only they didn't have any noodles. So, she'd taken change from the swear jar and hurried out of the apartment and down the stairs to the street below.

The grocery store was two blocks away. Two blocks and two alleys away. She had been in such a hurry she'd nearly tripped over a kitten. When she stopped to see if she'd hurt it, a man stepped out of the alley and snatched her from behind, clamped a hand over her mouth and dragged her into the shadows. No one heard her scream, no one came to help.

Pushing the nightmare to the back of her mind, Roxi smiled. "It's been a long time. I'm well over it."

"Then why don't you date? You've never had a steady boyfriend." The old army sergeant shook his head. "It's not natural."

"Oh, Frank. I'm fine. Just picky." And scared. Other than being raped at thirteen, she'd never been with a man. She read books and watched R-rated movies. She knew what was supposed to happen, but she wasn't sure how she'd react to having a man on top of her. For the first three years after the attack, she'd woken up in a panic when she got tangled in the sheets and couldn't get out.

Every time she got close to a man and even considered getting intimate, she'd panicked. Her heart raced, and she broke out in a cold sweat. Except last night.

Yes, she'd pushed Decker away, but not because she was in a panic, but because she was anticipating it and didn't want Decker to realize she was a freak.

When the usual anxiety attack didn't happen, it was too late. The moment had been lost.

"What about Decker?" Frank asked, breaking into Roxi's thoughts.

"What about him?" she asked, heat stealing into her cheeks.

"What's his story?"

"Like I said, I don't know much about him." *Just that his wife is dead, and he kisses like a dream.*

"I didn't know much about your mother when I fell in love with her. The same day we met, I knew."

Roxi faced Frank, crossing her arms over her chest. "Did you ever tell her that you loved her?"

The older man's shoulder lifted, but he refused to meet her gaze. "She made it pretty clear it was your father she preferred."

"What about after my father died and you brought us here to live?" Roxi asked. "Did you tell her then?"

"Angela had enough on her mind helping you deal with what happened and making a new life for the two of you. Then the cancer set in."

"You never told her." Roxi's arms fell to her sides and her chest hurt for the man who'd loved Angela Lanier and done everything to help her when her world fell apart. He'd been there when her mom had been diagnosed with stage IV ovarian cancer and sat at her bedside while she'd slowly slipped away. "She must have known. No man would have done that much for her if he didn't love her."

"It doesn't matter anymore." Frank nodded toward the window. "What matters is that you give yourself a chance to find love. Speaking of chances, Decker just left."

Roxi leaned over to look through the window into the bar. Decker's seat was empty. Otis padded into the kitchen and looked up at her.

"Did he leave you?" she asked and bent to pat the dog's head.

"That's all the supplies. I'll cover the bar if you want to take a break," Frank offered.

Roxi fought the desire to run out the door after Decker. She didn't want to appear too anxious to see him again. All she'd agreed to was a walk with Decker and Otis at three o'clock.

She glanced at the clock on the wall. She had fifteen minutes.

Her heart fluttered, and she glanced down at the old jeans and T-shirt she'd thrown on that morning when she'd been too sleepy to think straight.

"If you're sure..." she said, turning toward the exit, even as she spoke.

Frank chuckled. "Go"

Roxi walked out the back door. As soon as it shut behind her, she raced up the stairs and into her apartment above. She stripped out of the jeans and T-shirt, ran a brush through the knots in her hair and pulled it back in a messy bun that wouldn't last two minutes in the salty breeze. Then she stood in front of her closet, biting her lip.

Did she wear shorts? No, the wind had a bite to it today, though she knew her legs were one of her best features. She could wear the shorts and a long-sleeved, loose shirt. Then she spied the powder blue sundress she'd worn to a friend's wedding on the beach. With five minutes to get to the agreed upon location, she didn't have time to waste. She slipped the dress over her head and let it slide down over her body, the fabric loose and light. The matching cardigan would cover her arms and keep her from getting too cold. One last glance in the mirror and she hurried down the stairs, barefoot. Walking on the beach was best done without shoes. Otis followed behind her and bounded ahead, kicking up sand as he raced toward the pier.

Her heart thudding against her ribs, Roxi found herself skipping along after Otis. When she realized she was practically running, she slowed to a sedate walk, reining in the rising excitement. Where was he? All she could make out ahead was the tall, spindly poles of the pier and Otis barreling toward them.

Then movement on the sand before the pier made her heart stutter. Otis was attacking the figure and seemed to have him pinned to the ground.

Roxi ran toward them, her heart caught in her throat, her muscles and lungs burning. Her dog had been professionally trained to protect her. She'd seen him at the training center where she and Frank purchased him, viciously attacking upon command. "Otis! Down, boy!"

As she neared the dog and the man, she realized they were wrestling in the sand. Otis alternated between pretending to tear at Decker's arm and licking the man's face, his tail wagging like a puppy with a new friend.

Roxi stopped running and bent over, sucking air into her lungs. "Damn dog," she muttered when she could breathe again.

Decker rolled to his feet and brushed sand from his shirt, hair and shorts. "I think Otis and I have bonded."

Her lips twisted into a wry smile. "Some guard dog he turned out to be."

"I'm sure he'd be perfectly ferocious if he felt you were threatened." As if to prove Decker wrong, Otis rolled over in the sand for Decker to rub his belly.

"Yeah, ferocious." Roxi clicked her tongue. "Come on Rambo, let's go for that walk."

"Otis." Decker winked. "His name is Otis."

The dog rolled to his feet and shook sand all over them, before running beneath the pier and out the other side.

Roxi and Decker fell in step, walking in silence. They passed beneath the shadowy pier and back out into the sunshine.

Just two normal people having a friendly walk along the beach, Roxi tried to tell herself. She was emotionally scarred from being raped, and he still grieved for his dead wife. What did it hurt to live in an imaginary *normal* world, if only for a short time? It wasn't as if they were going to fall in bed and make mad passionate love in the middle of the day.

Well, damn. No sooner had the idea presented itself, then she imagined him stretched out on the sand, naked and waiting for her to straddle his big body.

"Why here?" she asked, curious about the man, and desperately trying to focus on anything but the way his broad shoulders filled out the T-shirt he wore.

"Pardon?" He shot a glance her way.

"Why did you decide to stay here?"

He walked along several more steps and bent to collect a shell from the wet sand. "I guess I was ready for a change." He straightened and handed her the perfectly formed shell with a spiral curve extending to a point, the inside a shiny, soft peachy-pink mother of pearl. "And you don't find sea shells on the sidewalks of a city." He slipped his hands into his pockets and continued walking. "What about you? Why here?"

She smoothed the sand off the shell and ran her finger over the slick surface, loving the smooth beauty of nature's work of art. "I've been here for the past fourteen years."

"So? You could have moved."

She swept her hands out and turned around. "Why would I leave all this?"

"Opportunity, a chance to see the rest of the world, view life outside a vacation town, avoid the cape winters." He shrugged. "Any number of reasons."

She stiffened. "I love the snow, and I have everything I need here."

"Everything?" he questioned. "You've never wanted to visit other places?"

Roxi shook her head. "I can look them up on the internet."

His brow wrinkled, and his lips twisted. "Some people would say you're hiding from the world."

Roxi stopped walking. "What is this, an inquisition?"

Decker took her hands in his. "No. I'm sorry. I'm just trying to understand you."

"I like it here." She pulled her hands from his. "It's the only place I've ever felt…." Dragging in a deep breath, she turned back the way they'd come. "It doesn't matter."

Decker stepped around and stood in front of her, blocking her path. He lifted her chin with one of his fingers and stared into her eyes, refusing to let her look away. "The only place you've ever felt *what,* Roxi?"

She turned her face toward the water, jerking away from his hand, her emotions intense, naked and raw. "It's the only place I've ever felt *safe.*"

CHAPTER 6

DECKER'S HEART clenched at the rawness of Roxi's voice, at the shadows darkening her pale blue eyes. "I'm sorry." He brushed the back of his knuckles across her cheek, wanting to pull her into his arms and hold her, to chase away whatever demons plagued her. Deep inside, he knew holding her would only make things worse.

His digging had opened a wound she apparently hadn't wanted exposed.

Otis returned to them and sat at Roxi's feet, nuzzling her hand at her side.

She stroked his head and stared down at the dog, her eyes filled, but no tears fell.

"Forget I asked." Decker stroked his fingers down her arm and lifted her hand, careful not to hold too tight. He brought her fingers to his lips and brushed a feather-soft kiss to the backs of her knuckles. "Please. Let's walk. I promise to keep my mouth shut."

He tugged her hand gently and turned to resume their walk down the beach. He angled toward the surf, his bare feet padding through the damp sand.

"You're right," Roxi said softly. "I have been hiding from the world."

Decker didn't respond, just glanced her way, giving her all the leeway to share whatever she wanted, or nothing at all.

"Since I came here, the Cape has been my sanctuary. I almost feel that if I leave, I'll disappear, or this place will disappear, and I won't be able to get back."

"How long has it been since you left the Cape area?"

She shrugged and kept walking. "I leave, every once in a while, for supplies or to visit friends, but I can't wait to get back."

"Why do you dislike the outside world so much?"

For a long moment, Roxi remained silent and then she said, "It doesn't matter. I never want to leave here."

The beautiful, seemingly self-assured owner of the Gone Fishin' Bar & Grill was afraid to leave the Cape.

Why?

Decker didn't press the issue. He wasn't even sure why he'd asked her out for a walk on the beach. He slowed to a stop and stared out at the water, churning in the afternoon sun. "I like the way the water is always in motion. I can watch it for hours." As if to emphasize his statement, he dropped to sit on the dry sand.

Roxi hesitated then sat beside him, pulled her knees up to her chin and wrapped her arms around her legs. "The waves are already getting bigger. The weatherman predicted we might get hit by the tropical storm headed up the coast."

Decker nodded. "The chances of it getting close enough to cause damage are pretty slim."

She stared out at the choppy water. "If you're worried, the state will call for evacuation before it hits."

"I'm not too worried. But what about you? Have you ever evacuated?" Decker asked.

Roxi nodded. "Frank, my mother and I have only evacuated two times over the past fourteen years. The coastline was hit several times in the same season. We had plenty of warning. Enough time to board up the bar and pack the important stuff into our cars before we joined the line of cars heading inland."

"Does your mother live around here now?" he asked.

Roxi didn't answer for a long moment. "My

mother died of cancer three years ago."

Decker drew in a deep breath. "I'm sorry for your loss." So, she had something in common with him. She'd lost someone she loved. Not that he wished that kind of loss on anyone, but he could feel the connection between them even more.

Otis ran back and dropped onto the sand beside Decker, panting loudly.

"I love to sit on the beach and stare out at the Cape and all its personalities," Roxi said.

Decker faced the water. "Personalities?"

"You know. Sunrise when everything is fresh from the night and the water is like glass, she's like a teenager on the verge of adulthood."

A smile tugged at his mouth. "That's one way to look at it."

An answering smile quirked at the corners of her lips. "And when the sun is bearing down, hot and relentless, she's a lounging lioness, basking in the rays, fat from feasting and lord of her domain."

"What about now?" Decker turned to watch the expressions play across Roxi's eyes.

Wind whipped her hair around her face and Roxi raised her hand to push it back, exposing a hint of a lacy white bra and the tantalizing swell of her breast beneath her powder-blue dress. With her legs drawn up, her bare calves flexed, the muscles taut and shapely. Though the dress covered her thighs, ass and body, it was sheer enough to give Decker a hint of what lay beneath the soft fabric.

Flame shot straight to Decker's groin and he fought to control himself and keep from sprouting a tent in his shorts.

Her gaze went to the sea. Roxi went on, unaware of the picture she presented or of the reaction Decker's body gave in response. "Right now, she's on the verge of discovery, tempted by change and tempting in her tempestuousness."

Decker chuckled. "That's an old-fashioned word."

"But it fits her." She faced him. "Don't you see it?" Her gaze was as intense as the constant churning of the sea and just as beautiful.

"I see it," he said, wanting more than anything to reach out, cup her face and kiss those full sensuous lips. "You're amazing."

Roxi laughed, her cheeks blooming with color. "You probably think I'm a flake."

"No. I think you see things differently." He hurried to add, "In a good way."

She sighed. "Even when the seas are rough, I find comfort in them."

"Why don't you feel safe outside of Cape Cod?" As soon as the words were out of his mouth, Decker wished he could take them back.

Her back stiffened and the light faded from her

eyes. “I just don’t.” Roxi glanced at the watch on Decker’s wrist. “What time is it?”

“A quarter to five.”

“Shoot.” She scrambled to her feet, brushing sand from her backside. “I have to get back and help Frank manage the dinner crowd.”

Decker rose to stand beside her and reached for her hand, holding it lightly in his own. “I’m glad you came for a walk with me. I haven’t walked on a beach with a woman for a very long time.”

Her gaze locked with his. “Since your wife died?”

He nodded.

Roxi’s brows puckered. “You must have loved her a great deal.”

“I did.” His glance dropped to where their hands touched. “But I have to get on with my life.”

Roxi lifted her other hand to cup his face, stepping close enough Decker could smell the fragrant scent of her hair. “Yes, you do. You have a lot to offer some lucky woman.”

He chuckled and shook his head. “I have too much baggage.”

“Not, really. You’re not bad to look at, and you seem nice. Or at least you’ve been nice to me.”

“It’s easy to be nice to you.”

Roxi leaned closer and pecked him on the cheek, her lips brushing lightly, barely a whisper across his skin.

Before she could back away, he turned his face and swept his lips across hers, his free hand cupping the back of her neck, applying a slight pressure to bring her closer.

Her body grew rigid, then relaxed, melting against him, her hand rising to rest against his chest, her touch burning a path straight through to his heart.

Then she turned and ran, Otis racing after her, barking.

Decker stood rooted in the sand until Roxi and Otis disappeared beneath the shadowy pier.

That kiss had cost him. No longer could he cling to the memory of Allison and wallow in the self-inflicted guilt that had kept him celibate for the past two years. He couldn't continue to bury himself in solitude, not when the troubled gaze of a beautiful bar owner and the tingling sensation of her kiss lingered on his mind and lips.

BY THE TIME Roxi arrived at the bar, she was panting, and her heart raced, not only from the sprint, but also from the realization that she'd kissed a man for the second time, and hadn't felt smothered or forced in any way. Which left her feeling baffled, anxious and twitchy. If it felt so good, why had she run?

The freedom of that kiss and the way her body begged for more, was so foreign to her that it had both frightened and excited her at once. Instead of entering through the front door of the bar, she rounded the building and stood outside the back entrance, pressing her palms to her heated cheeks.

Wow. In her head, she repeated that one word. *Wow.*

She was torn between getting back to her normal life and running all the way back down the beach and into Decker's arms for more of the magic that lifted her long-running trepidation over intimacy. Not only did she like the kiss, it inspired a desire that swept over her, making her want so much more. And they'd kissed in broad daylight... on a public beach. She could imagine how much more sensuous a kiss in the moonlight might be and wanted to test the theory.

Roxi stood at the bottom of the staircase leading up to her little apartment, frozen in thought. Would kissing Decker in the darkness remind her too much of when she'd been attacked?

Roxi shook her head. *No.* She'd been with him in the moonlight the night before and hadn't felt the least bit threatened. Granted, they'd just survived a wicked riptide and neither one of them had the energy to do anything else besides breathe and let their muscles rest from the strain of swimming to shore.

Hell, she was overthinking everything about the man. With a business to run, she couldn't stand around daydreaming about the hot guy on the beach. She led Otis up the stairs, gave him fresh water and a bowl of his favorite dog food. Knowing she had a bar to run, she slipped out of the blue dress and into her cutoffs and tank top. With a sigh, she headed down to the kitchen entrance. As she reached for the doorknob, the back door opened, almost hitting her in the face.

"Oh, there you are." Frank carried a bag of trash. "Four customers just walked in, and Marcy is still sick, leaving only you and me to cover the bar."

"Oh, dear. I hope she'll be okay." Ducking her head, Roxi squeezed past Frank. "I'd better go see what they want."

Frank's free hand shot out and captured Roxi's arm. "Are you okay?"

Roxi gave him a round-eyed, innocent look. "Sure. Why wouldn't I be?" Other than she'd had an amazing kiss and her heart wouldn't slow down, she was perfectly fine. Better than fine.

"Your cheeks are kind of red." He pressed the back of his hand to her forehead. "You're not catching what Marcy has, are you?"

"No. No. I feel fine." Amazing. Alive. Perhaps for the first time since she was thirteen.

"Well, take it easy tonight, just in case."

"Mondays are usually slow at the end of the summer season. No worries." She entered the Gone Fishin' Bar, hurried to wash her hands and grabbed an order pad and pen before going to work. The next couple of hours passed like molasses in the winter. When she glanced at the clock on the wall, it seemed as though the hands hadn't budged. Every time the door opened, she looked up, her pulse increasing with the hope in the back of her mind that it might be Decker in his shorts and polo shirt, his dark hair mussed from the wind, a smile on his lips.

Each time disappointment slowed her heart rate when it wasn't Decker. She pasted a smile on her lips and waited on the customers eager for a meal and libations to enhance their Cape experience.

Food and drink weren't what had enhanced Roxi's Cape life. One tall, dark and incredibly handsome widower had done the trick and she could hardly wait until he showed up at the bar.

Eventually, Roxi got too busy filling orders and cleaning tables to check the door every five minutes. As one hour passed into the next, the crowd of dinner guests thinned to the people there to watch the Monday night football games on the four televisions mounted in the corners.

Roxi had just returned from taking a tub of dirty dishes to the kitchen when she spotted Decker taking a seat at the bar.

Her heart skipped several beats, and she fought the urge to check her hair. She smoothed her hands over her denim cutoffs and slipped behind the bar, pasting a subdued smile on her face when she wanted to grin like an idiot. Inside, she could be as giddy as a teenager with a crush. On the outside, she didn't want to appear too eager. Hell, she hadn't done a lot of dating, and what did she know about what men liked or didn't like?

Awkward and suddenly insecure, her hands shook. She grabbed a rag and wiped it across the counter to where he sat. "Hi."

"Hey."

The dead air stretched between them until Roxi found her tongue. "What can I get you?" She held up her hand. "Let me guess—scotch on the rocks?"

He nodded, a real smile tilting his lips upward. "Thanks."

She bent to grab the bottle of scotch from beneath the counter, dropped ice into a tumbler and poured. "Have you eaten? Do you want a menu?" Grabbing the rag, she wiped the counter again, trying to keep busy so that he didn't notice how nervous she was.

"I had a sandwich at my place." He reached out and placed his hand over hers. "Roxi, I didn't come for dinner. I wanted to know if you were walking Otis after work tonight and, assuming you were, if you'd mind company."

Her stomach erupted in a flock of butterflies all fluttering at once. "Um. Yes. I usually walk Otis before I call it a night." Her cheeks flooded with heat and, low in her core, her insides tightened. "And yes, I would like company."

He nodded. "Good."

"Hey, sweetheart," one of the men watching the game called out. "Can we get a refill on this pitcher?" He held up the empty pitcher.

Roxi tamped down her irritation at being called sweetheart and answered, "Sure." She hated leaving Decker at the bar but hurried to fill the order and take another. The football teams were playing a close game and the noise in the bar increased as the men downed their fifth pitcher of beer and the game headed into the fourth quarter.

Roxi waited on a couple having a late dinner of buffalo wings and fries, refilling their drinks before she moved to the big table of game watchers to clean up the empty mugs and plates of snacks.

As she turned with the tray of dirty dishes and trash, the man who'd called her sweetheart, grabbed her around the middle and swung her into his lap. The tray she'd been holding crashed to the floor, the contents scattering, the heavy glass mugs hitting hard. One shattered, shooting broken shards of glass across the room.

Anger shot through Roxi and she struggled to stand. "Sir, let go of me."

"Ah, sweetheart, I just want a little kiss. Just one." He wrapped his hands in her hair and pulled hard, forcing her to lie back on his lap.

The surprise of the assault had caught her off guard, and the added pressure to lie across his lap made her heart race and the first stirrings of panic to flare. That helpless feeling she'd had when she'd been thirteen washed over her. Once again, she was a young teen attacked by a man three times her weight and forced into a back alley. She drew in a deep breath, reminding herself she wasn't that kid, and said as calmly as she could, "Let go of me."

The man leaned over her, his breath smelling of the many mugs of beer he'd guzzled over the past few hours. "Just one kiss, baby. That's all. Just one."

"Come on Len, let the girl go," one of his buddies said.

Her fists clenched, Roxi turned her face to avoid the bastard's lips connecting with hers. If he didn't let go of her at the count of three, she'd slam the heel of her palm into his nose. One...two...

Before Roxi could swing her arm, Len lurched to his feet, releasing his hold on her hair.

Roxi rolled to the floor and scrambled to her feet, braced for a fight.

Len stumbled backward, his chair crashing to the floor. He was propelled across the room by a stern-faced Decker, marching him to the exit.

Frank hurried ahead and flung the door open.

Decker charged through, holding the man's arm jacked up between his shoulder blades.

"I'll have you up on charges!" Len shouted between cries of pain. "I know my rights."

"Yeah, and you gave them up when you violated Roxi's," Decker said, his voice low and angry.

Roxi followed the crowd gathered around the two men on the front porch of the Gone Fishin' Bar & Grill.

Decker gave the man a shove and let go of his arm.

Len staggered toward the steps leading off the porch.

"Show's over," Decker called out and turned toward the remaining crowd gathered around to watch.

Instead of descending the stairs, Len spun and charged at Decker like a linebacker going after a quarterback.

"Decker, look out!" Roxi cried.

He'd only turned halfway around when Len hit him in the side with his shoulder, slamming him up against the wall. But Decker recovered sooner than Len and jammed his elbow into his attacker's gut.

Len doubled over and staggered backward.

Frank grabbed Len's arms from behind and walked him down the steps. "You're not welcome here anymore. Don't come back." Then he shoved Len, sending him flying into the sand.

His buddies laughed. One of them went down to help him to his feet.

Len slapped his friend's hands away and lurched to his feet, swaying. "I'll go wherever I damn well please."

Roxi stood at the top of the stairs, her feet spread wide, her hands fisted on her hips. "That's fine, as long as you don't come back to the Gone Fishin' Bar & Grill."

DECKER STOOD TALL at her side. Amazed at how strong and proud she was in the face of such an attack.

"Come on, Len," his friend said. "It's not worth it."

"That's right, get him out of here before I call the police," Frank warned.

"I'm leaving, but I'm not through with you," Len pointed his finger at Decker.

Decker stepped down one step, balling his fists. "Yes. You are."

"We're leaving," Len's friend said, dragging at the man's arm.

Decker remained on the step, ready to take on any other dumbass who dared to manhandle Roxi. Once the crowd cleared, he turned to Roxi. "Are you okay?"

Her stiff shoulders sagged, and she nodded. "I hate when men think a woman is nothing more than a piece of meat."

Frank put an arm around her and hugged her. "You sure you're all right?"

She smiled at Frank and then at Decker. "I am, thanks to you two."

Frank shook his head. "Nah, I saw you. If Decker hadn't stepped in when he did, you'd have floored that jerk with a fist to the nose." His chest puffed out. "You make me proud."

"I should have done it sooner, I just didn't relish cleaning blood off the floor."

"You don't worry about the blood. Just do what you have to." Frank hugged her again "Come on. I think we can close early tonight. Especially after all the excitement."

Roxi entered the bar and went to work cleaning up for the night. If her hands shook, she scrubbed harder, swept faster and hurried through the chores.

Decker stacked chairs on the tabletops and mopped after Roxi swept. Frank handled the kitchen, and within thirty minutes they had the bar cleaned and the lights turned off. The three of them exited through the rear entrance.

"Well, goodnight, Roxi." Frank kissed her cheek and hugged her briefly. "You sure you're going to be all right tonight? Want me to camp out on your couch?"

Roxi shook her head. "I'll be fine. I have Otis."

Frank nodded. "Then good night. And remember, you're not that thirteen-year-old kid anymore.

You could have taken that dumbass with one hand tied behind your back."

She nodded. "I know."

Frank climbed into his pickup and drove away to his cottage two miles down the road.

Which left Roxi with Decker. The shakes she'd experienced in the aftermath of the earlier attack started all over again. Only this time, she trembled in anticipation of the good things that might come of the rest of the night—if she played her cards right and didn't freeze at the man's touch. Decker made her feel incredibly sexy, desirable and... normal. In Roxi's books, normal was nirvana.

Come on, nirvana.

CHAPTER 7

DECKER STAYED by Roxi's side, the anger simmering beneath the surface. How he wished he'd driven a fist into Len's face for taking advantage of Roxi. The panic in her eyes had twisted at his heart. And what had Frank meant when he'd said she wasn't a helpless thirteen-year-old anymore? Roxi had told him she'd moved to Cape Cod when she was thirteen.

Which led Decker to believe something traumatic had occurred to precipitate her mother and Frank moving her to the coastal town. Had she been attacked?

His fist clenched even tighter thinking about the drunk pawing at her. Having been traumatized as a teen could still be affecting Roxi even today, and would explain why she ran away from him that afternoon when he'd kissed her.

His chest tightened, and his gut clenched. Damn. He could have frightened her as much as the drunk. "Look, Roxi. I'll understand if you don't feel comfortable walking with me tonight."

She turned to him, her brows furrowed. "Are you too tired?"

"No, not at all. It's just that after what happened earlier, you might not want to be with me, or any man for that matter."

Roxi scowled. "Otis needs a walk, and I won't let a drunk scare me so much that I refuse to come out of my house."

"Yeah, but walking after dark has its own set of dangers. If that nutcase decides to seek revenge on you because you wounded his pride, Frank and I might not be around to help you."

She lifted her chin. "I didn't need your help tonight. I could have taken care of myself, and I was about to do just that when you interfered."

He bowed slightly, a smile tugging at his lips. "My apologies."

"You laugh, but I've taken several self-defense lessons. I know how to immobilize a man." She curled her fingers and shot the heel of her palm toward Decker's nose stopping short of connecting. "A swift palm slammed upward on the nose drives the cartilage into the attacker's skull and could kill him. At the least, it hurts a great deal and causes the attacker's eyes to tear profusely, giving the victim a chance to escape."

Decker held up his hands in surrender. "Okay. I'm a believer. I hope you never have to use that technique on me." He glanced toward the top of the stairs. "I think I hear Otis scratching up there. We should rescue him before he destroys the door."

Roxi's shoulders relaxed, and she led the way up to her apartment. "I'm sorry if I come across too strong. I'm just passionate about defending myself. I don't ever want to be in a position of complete helplessness again." She shoved her key into the lock and let Otis out.

The dog bounded out before Decker could ask Roxi what she meant by "again." He wanted to know what caused her to be so guarded and why she was so determined to defend herself. Maybe with time, she'd open up and let him in. For now, it was enough to walk with her along the beach. Enough for him.

For the entire day, he hadn't thought about Allison, the wreck, or how he wished he'd gone with her when she'd died. Today he felt as though he might still be there for a reason. Whether it was to pull the jerk off Roxi in the Gone Fishin' bar or to walk along the beach with her, he didn't know. But something had changed in him from the moment they'd both beaten the riptide.

Roxi locked her apartment door and followed Otis down the steps. "Otis. Heel."

The German shepherd spun and returned to her side walking along, barely containing his energy. When they stepped out on the open beach, Roxi said. "Okay, Otis. You can play."

The dog shot ahead. The wind had picked up even more, whipping Roxi's hair about her head. A shiver shook her body, and she stepped closer to Decker.

"The national weather channel is tracking Hurricane Charlie. The outer edges of the storm are expected to skim the D.C. area tonight," Decker said, just to be talking.

Roxi slipped her hand into his and leaned against his shoulder. "If it doesn't hit the coast soon, it might make it up to us. We could get the call to evacuate tomorrow. In which case, Frank and I will be busy boarding the windows and packing up."

Decker liked how soft her fingers were inside his. At the same time, her hands and arms were strong, well-toned with muscles from working in the bar, carrying heavy trays and pushing a broom and a mop night after night. "I guess I'll be locking the storm shutters on the cottage, and I promised my neighbor I'd look after his cottage as well if the storm worsened."

"The traffic will back up on the road out. If they

call for evacuation, you'll want to get out as early as possible." She tossed her hair out of her face and stumbled in the sand.

"Thanks." He squeezed her fingers, gently, let go and slipped his arm around her waist, amused at their talk of weather when there was so much more going on between them. "I'll keep that in mind." Decker liked how she fit against him and was glad she didn't pull away.

They passed the pier and kept walking until they arrived at Decker's cottage.

"You don't have to walk me back to my apartment." Roxi stepped away from him. "Otis and I get along pretty well on our own."

He grinned. "I admire independent women. But would you consider coming in for a drink? I have beer in the refrigerator." His grin twisted wryly. "Though I'd think working in a bar, you'd be tired of just about every alcoholic drink."

Roxi smiled. "Ice water would be nice."

"I can do that." He waved her toward the stairs leading up to his cottage perched on thick treated posts, buried deep in the ground, made to weather the strongest storms and tides as high as twelve feet.

Otis slipped past them on their way up and sprawled on the decking at the top.

"I'd suggest sitting out on the deck, but the wind is really getting wicked. However, the living area overlooks the beach." Decker opened the door and held it for her to enter, followed by Otis.

"No, Otis!" Roxi grabbed his collar. "You weren't invited."

"He's welcome to come in."

Roxi released the dog's collar and stepped into the cottage.

Decker was surprised that having Roxi in his cottage didn't inspire the usual twinge of guilt he'd felt every time he considered seeing other women after Allison's death. Perhaps being at Cape Cod had helped him to let go. He'd never brought Allison here. This place held no shared memories. The cottage, the beach, the quaint towns were a clean slate for new memories. He found himself eager to create new ones with Roxi—a woman as different from Allison as he could imagine.

With Roxi in his cottage, all manners of possibilities raced through his head, and his heartbeat thudded against his chest. He felt like a teen on his first date and feared he'd make a mistake and scare her away. Fighting back the urge to take her into his arms and hold her, Decker strode past her to the kitchen and filled two wine glasses with ice and water. When he returned to the living area, Roxi stood at the huge picture windows, staring out at the night sky.

"It's hard to believe there's a hurricane off the coast when the moon is shining bright where we are." She accepted the wine glass and smiled. "Nice touch."

"It's our first drink together." He touched the rim of his glass to hers. "To getting to know each other."

She tilted her glass, sipped the water and then set it on a nearby end table. With a determined look, she took his glass from his hand, set it beside hers and then stood in front of him. "I've not been in many relationships, so I might get this all wrong…but…the kiss yesterday…" She bit her lip, her cheeks flooding with color.

Decker waited. Roxi's confession and confusion were endearing. He wanted anything that happened to be something *she* wanted and initiated. If she had been sexually assaulted as a young teen, she might still have issues with men.

With every ounce of control he could muster, he held back and let *her* come to *him*. At the same time, he understood the weight of her decision if she chose to initiate something with him. It meant Decker had to be open for more than a one-night-stand. He had to let go of the grief and guilt he'd harbored since Allison's death.

His gut clenched for a moment as his insides churned. Allison was gone. What they'd had as husband and wife had been good. They'd been happy.

It was quite possible the beautiful woman in

front of him had as many hang-ups as he did. Was Decker the right person for her? Would he get cold feet and back out if she wanted more than a kiss? She deserved someone whole, committed, sure of his intentions and gentle.

But, damn it, he couldn't turn away. Not when she stared at him with big cornflower blue eyes, so wide, trusting and—holy shit—sexy!

THE MOMENT DECKER yanked Len out of his seat and threw him out the door of the Gone Fishin' Bar & Grill, Roxi knew that John Decker was the kind of guy she could trust. He would never do anything to hurt her. Most likely, he'd leap into any fray to protect her. As she stood in front of him, her pulse beat a wicked tattoo against her eardrums, pushing red-hot blood through her veins to pool low in her belly. A delicious ache built at the juncture of her thighs.

"What was I saying?" Her heart beat so fast, it made her a little dizzy. Or was it the ultra-male scent of Decker and his aftershave? Roxi swayed toward him, her hands reaching out to settle against his rock-hard chest.

"Something about a kiss." He leaned closer.

"Oh." The heat in her cheeks deepened. "Yes… uh…did I say thank you for saving me from that jerk tonight?"

Decker raised his hands to rest on her arms. He didn't hold her tight, giving her every opportunity to shrug free. "Not actually." Brushing a strand of hair behind her ear, he chuckled. "I gathered you were a little disappointed you didn't get to use your ninja talents on the guy."

Her back stiffened. She preferred to fight her own battles, if for no other reason than to prove she could. "Well, I *could* have taken him out. But it worked out for the best. No blood to clean up is always a good thing." Roxi stared at his chest, afraid that if she looked into his eyes, she'd forget her name, much less what she wanted to say before she chickened out.

"And your point about the kiss?" he prompted, touching a finger to her chin, lifting it, forcing her to look him square in the eyes.

She fell into his green-eyed gaze, her own unflinching, though her cheeks burned and her core flamed. "Why did you kiss me?"

He blinked and answered without hesitation, "I wanted to so badly, I *had* to."

Her brows V'd toward the bridge of her nose and a sick feeling filled her belly. "Do I remind you of your wife?"

Decker shook his head, brushing a hand along her cheek. "No. Not in the least. She had short, dark hair, brown eyes and pale skin."

Almost opposite of Roxi's light blond hair and blue eyes. Her skin had the soft, healthy golden tan of one who enjoyed the outdoors as much as possible.

Decker's brows rose. "Why did *you* kiss *me*?" He stepped closer, his fingers resting on her arms.

Holy hell, she wanted him to pull her against him. Her gaze slid to his lips and her tongue snaked out to moisten her suddenly dry lips. "I kissed you because…because…" she sighed, "because I couldn't *not* kiss you." She touched her fingers to his chest and whispered, "And I want to do it all again." Her confession left her open, exposed and vulnerable.

Decker's fingers tightened on her arms, but he didn't haul her against his body. "Are you sure? The last time we kissed you ran off like a scalded cat."

She curled her fingers into his shirt tugging him closer. "I promise not to run this time."

"Why *did* you run? Did I do something to scare you?" He stroked his hands down her arms, sending tingles across her nerve endings.

Roxi, the tough bar owner shook her head, her eyes rounded, a tremor shaking her beneath his hands. Obviously, she wasn't as tough as she thought she was. Hell, she was shaking, afraid he'd turn away and leave her standing there after confessing she wanted to kiss him again.

What was his question? She blinked and thought before answering, "No, of course you don't scare me." She snorted softly. "I scare myself." Her gaze dropped to where her hands twisted in the fabric of his shirt. "You see, I've never felt that… that…intensity of desire as I did when I kissed you."

"And it scared you?" He traced his finger up her arm, across her shoulder and cupped her cheek. "Do you want to kiss me again and see if you're still scared."

She gave him a tremulous smile. "Could I?"

"Darlin' you don't even have to ask." He bent until his mouth hovered over hers, allowing her to close the distance.

When she did, her control slipped, and she wrapped her arms around his neck, dragging him closer.

His hands curled around her hips and pulled her against him. If she'd had doubt about his attraction to her, she didn't after his erection pressed into the softness of her belly, and she could think of even better places for him to press into. She closed her eyes, reminding herself to take it slowly.

Roxi was a badass on the outside, but on the inside, she was as vulnerable as a virgin and she didn't want to scare him away with her inept sexual abilities.

HOLY HELL. Decker held her like a china doll, afraid he'd break her if he wasn't careful. Was he ready for this kind of commitment? She deserved a man who wasn't as screwed up as he was. Decker wasn't sure he wanted anything more than a roll in the sheets. He wasn't over the death of his wife and the survivor's guilt he'd lived with since.

Roxi laced her fingers through his hair, urging him closer.

He couldn't resist. Decker traced the seam of her lips and she opened to him. He swept in, claiming her tongue in a long, sensuous thrust.

Her breasts pressed against his chest and she moaned into his mouth.

The sound spiked his arousal, shooting a bolt of electricity straight to his groin. He skimmed her lower back and downward over the curve of her ass, cupping her cheeks in his palms.

She shifted, parting her legs to straddle one of his, the apex of her thighs rubbing over his taut muscle.

The tension stretched tight, Decker's grasp on control teetered on the verge of complete abandon. If he didn't stop now, he wouldn't be able to, and he knew it had to be Roxi's choice for how far they did or didn't go. Coming on too strong, pushing her up against the wall and taking her in the middle of the living room could frighten her and make her run again. Sure, she'd said she'd scared herself, but how much of that fear had to do with how aroused he'd obviously been?

Though it took all of his concentration, Decker pulled away first and pressed his forehead to hers, his breathing ragged, his heart thudding against his ribs. "If this is as far as you want to go, tell me now. If we go any farther, I can't guarantee I can stop making love to you."

"Who said I wanted to stop?" She bunched her fingers in the fabric of his shirt, dragged it out of the waistband of his trousers and pushed it up over his head.

Decker tossed it to the side and curled his fingers around her hips.

Roxi ran her hands over his bare chest, the tip of her tongue darting out to moisten her lips. "Your muscles are so hard."

He captured one of her hands. "Darlin', you're killing me."

She stared at her hands on his chest. "Because I'm touching you?"

"Hell, Roxi. Just being with you makes me crazy."

"Crazy good or crazy bad?" She twirled her finger around one of his small brown nipples.

Decker groaned. "Crazy good, in a way that makes me want to be bad."

She leaned forward and kissed the nipple. "What if I want you to be crazy bad?"

"I don't want to scare you."

She trailed her fingers down his chest, across his abs to the rivet on his jeans. "Then let me get this party started."

"Okay. I'm all for you taking the lead." He raised

his hands in surrender. "As long as you tell me when, or if, we're going too fast."

She gave him a half-smile. "Thanks."

Anything that would move toward the possibility of getting naked with Roxi was all right in Decker's books. God, he hoped that's where she was headed, or he might explode.

Roxi took his hand and led him toward the open bedroom door.

Decker squeezed her fingers, excitement building inside.

Once through the door, Roxi turned to face him and dragged her tank top up over her head and let it drop to the floor. A shiver rippled across her body as she stood in front of him in her bra and cutoffs. She flicked the rivet through the button hole on his jeans and tugged his zipper down.

His erection sprang free into the palm of her hand.

Roxi curled her fingers around him, her eyes widening. "Wow, are you always this big and hard."

"Jesus, Roxi." Decker gripped her arms and clenched his jaw to keep from tossing her on the bed and making insanely passionate love to her. He closed his eyes and drew in a deep, steadying breath. "No, I'm not always this way. Only when a beautiful woman wraps herself around me." He tipped her chin up, forcing her to look him in the eyes. "Darlin', have you never made love with a man?"

A shadow crossed over her face, her pale blue eyes darkening, and she closed her eyes. "I'm not a virgin, if that's what you mean," she said softy.

"Roxi, look at me," Decker said softly. "You didn't answer me. Not really."

She opened her eyes, her brow puckering, her fingers releasing him. "I've been with a man before." Her voice was low, and hard.

He cupped her cheek. "I take it you didn't consent."

"No." She stepped back and spun away, her arms wrapped around her bare middle. "I was raped."

Red hot anger seared through Decker. "The bastard deserves to die." Tucking himself back into his jeans, he zipped, leaving the rivet unbuttoned. He gripped her arms and pulled her back to his chest, holding her lightly, allowing her the option of escaping easily. "I'm sorry," he whispered against her hair. "Have you been with a man since?"

"No." She waved her hand and let it drop to her side. "Every time a man tried to make love to me afterward, I panicked."

"Have you shared your fears with any other man?"

She stiffened. "No."

His heart fluttered. She'd told him. That had to mean something.

"Maybe what you need is to be in control. If you *want* to make it happen, take charge in the situation."

"What if I do something stupid?" She stared out at the moonlit sky.

He took her hand and raised it to his lips. "You can't do anything stupid. You're a strong, independent woman."

"To a certain extent." Roxi faced him. "I've hidden myself away on this island for so long, but I haven't been idle or a recluse by any means."

"You're friendly with your customers, and they love you."

She grimaced. "Yeah, except that Len who was such a butt." Roxi sighed, stared out the window again, and went on, her words short and emphasized. "The point is, I'm a business owner and I deal with people all day and night. I should be confident enough in my own abilities to enjoy a reasonable sex life."

"Hey, I won't argue that point." He grinned. "I have a lot at stake here."

Her shoulders relaxed as she faced him again, a wry smile twisting her lips. "Thanks for being patient with me."

He intertwined his fingers with hers. "Tell you what, if you still want to get down and dirty, I'll do my best not to interfere too much. I'm all for equal opportunity, as well. You can be on top."

She laughed out loud and touched his chest. "Are you always this accommodating?"

"Honey, you have no idea how difficult it is to keep from holding you so tight you can't get away. I want you in the worst way."

"Then we're not stopping now?" Roxi said, a smile spreading across her face.

"Not unless *you* want to. But you're in charge, and I'll do anything you want me to, within reason, of course."

"You mean that?" She stared up into his eyes, her own round, trusting.

"I do." He spread his arms wide. "I won't touch you, unless you ask."

"Would you touch me now?" she asked.

He chuckled. "So soon?"

Her blue eyes darkened. "The sooner, the better."

Decker dragged his finger along the curve of her jaw, down the long straight column of her neck and across her collar bone. He glanced up to gauge her reaction as his hand drew near the swell of her breast in the lacy white bra.

Her gaze fixed on the hand gliding across the plump swell of her breast.

"Tell me to stop, and I will," he said, praying she wouldn't.

"Stop."

Decker's fingers froze on the edge of the lacy undergarment.

Roxi reached behind her and flicked the hooks on her bra, releasing them. Then she shimmied the rest of the way out and tossed the bra over the nightstand. "Now, where were we?"

Decker's heart leaped, and his erection jerked.

Roxi raised one of Decker's hands and laid it across her shoulder. "I hope I didn't kill the mood."

"You couldn't," he said, his voice strained from pulling way back on the reins. "Not the way I'm feeling right now."

Once again, her fingers traced down the front of Decker's torso and farther south to the zipper he'd just pulled up.

Roxi eased it down again. This time, when he poked out of the denim, she paused briefly to fondle him and then pushed his jeans downward.

Decker toed off his boots and stepped clear of his jeans. Naked in front of her, he reached for the waistband of her cutoffs. With his fingers on the button, he caught her gaze. "Are you okay with this?"

She nodded. "I'd feel a whole lot better if I were naked too." She grinned and guided his hand to the button, helping him release it.

He shoved her shorts over her rounded hips and followed them down to her ankles. Decker dropped to one knee and helped her step out. Then he caressed her ankles, brushing his fingers along the insides of her legs, rounding to the backs of her knees and skimming the tenderness of her inner thighs.

He'd show her that making love was completely different than having a man force himself on her.

CHAPTER 8

ROXI SUCKED IN A BREATH, her heart hammering in her chest. The closer his fingers moved toward her center, the weaker her knees grew until they wobbled, refusing to hold her upright. She placed her hands on Decker's shoulders to steady herself.

God, he was beautiful—his body hard, tanned and sexy. And his cock was thick, jutting out like a sword to pierce her.

A shiver rippled over her body and that familiar ache built at her center, spreading outward to every nerve ending in her body, making her ultra-sensitive to his touch. When he swept his fingers across the triangle of fabric covering her sex, she moaned.

Immediately his hand stopped, and he glanced up, his brows furrowed. "Are you still okay with this?"

She nodded, biting on her lower lip, her entire

body burning with desire, eager for him to take it to the next step.

And he did. Slipping his finger into the elastic waistband of her panties, he dragged them down.

Impatience made Roxi help things along, quickly shucking the constricting garment. Free of all clothing and wanting him inside her, she grabbed his hand and backed toward the bed.

When she bumped into the mattress with her bottom and the backs of her legs, heat rose in her cheeks. This was it. The first time she'd have sex with a man since she was thirteen. She'd avoided it with all the boys she'd dated from high school and beyond, until now. Every one of them gave up on her when she refused to go beyond second base. Either that, or she'd stopped answering their phone calls or told them she was busy until they quit calling.

The master of avoiding the inevitable, Roxi was glad she'd waited. With Decker standing naked in front of her, the possibility of making love never appealed to her more.

Holy hell, he was freakin' hot. She could stare at his naked form for hours and never get tired of seeing all those toned muscles and hard planes. Her core tightened in anticipation of his rigid staff gliding into her channel.

Oh, sweet Jesus, let it be soon!

Decker slid his hands around her middle and down over her bottom. He scooped her up.

Her legs naturally wrapped around his waist, her entrance poised over the tip of his cock. She tried to ease down over him.

Decker shook his head. "Not yet. I haven't even started the foreplay."

"I've heard foreplay is overrated," she said, her voice breathy, her breasts pressing against him. His chest hairs tickled, making her even more aware of every part of him touching her.

He laid her on the bed and pressed his lips to hers in a brief kiss. "We also need protection."

She bit her lip. How could she forget? After she'd been raped, she'd waited for two weeks, wracked with worry that she might be pregnant. At thirteen, she knew she was in no way ready to be a mother. Roxi had never been happier to start her period. She'd cried in the bathroom at school, embarrassed and relieved at once.

She'd felt dirty after the man had forced himself on her. Embarrassed, frightened, ashamed and violated. Although the man had said he'd kill her if she told anyone, she couldn't hide it from her mother. As soon as Roxi's mom came home from work, she knew something was wrong. Finding her daughter curled on the floor of the bathroom, bawling, was a sure sign all was not right in Roxi's world. Her mother had wrapped her arms around her and taken her to the hospital.

Roxi suffered the humiliation of the rape kit and recounting her story to a female police officer. Unfortunately, her attacker had never been caught.

Roxi pushed thoughts of that day to the very back of her mind and focused on the man standing beside the bed in all his naked glory. This was not a dirty bastard preying on young girls foolish enough to walk alone at night.

Decker was a man who knew how to please a woman in the most sensual way. And he was about to unleash his techniques on her. He slid onto the bed beside her and leaned on one elbow. “Still okay?”

She nodded. “But does it always take this long to get to the point?”

He grinned and brushed a strand of her hair out of her face. “Sometimes longer. You can’t rush perfection.” Then he winked.

Her heart fluttered and her skin tingled.

“You’re an incredibly beautiful woman.”

Roxi didn’t think of herself as beautiful. Passably pretty, but not beautiful. But when Decker looked at her like he was at that moment, with hunger in his eyes and an intensity that was hard to resist, Roxi felt sexy, desirable and incredibly feminine.

Decker tucked the hair behind her ear and

dragged his knuckles across her chin and lips, then drew a path down the length of her neck to the swells of her breasts. He paused to lightly pinch the tip of one nipple.

Roxi's back arched off the bed as if of its own accord. She touched the apex of her thighs, pressing down to sooth the ache growing at her core. No amount of pressure would ease the torment. She realized the only cure would be to take all of Decker into her to fill the void. And how she wished he'd get to that part soon. She wasn't certain how much more foreplay she could stand and not come apart.

Leaning over her, Decker sucked one of her nipples into his mouth, tongued and nibbled it until Roxi whimpered, her body on fire, her control slipping with every passing moment.

As if aware of his effect on her, Decker didn't linger over her breasts. He kissed his way over her ribs and across her belly, arriving at the tuft of hair over her sex.

Roxi parted her legs, letting him slide between them, a little shocked and completely turned on by what he was doing to her. Sure, she'd read erotic romances where men touched their women in the most private of places. But she'd never been the recipient of such tender caresses.

He parted her folds and stroked her with one of his fingers, drawing a line down to her entrance.

Her belly clenched, and she moaned again.

His warm chuckle breathed air over her heated entrance. "Like that?"

"Oh, sweet Jesus. Yes!" In the fading portion of her brain, she thought she should be embarrassed by her outburst, but when his tongue followed his finger, stroking the little nubbin of flesh, all thoughts exploded in a cacophony of sensations, threads of lightning bolting throughout her body.

She tensed, her back arched and she forgot to breathe. "Please," she whispered.

He touched her again, his tongue laving her, pushing her over the edge, past the brink of everything she'd ever known. Roxi dug her fingers into his hair and cried, "Decker!" Her body shook with the force of her release, and she rode the waves all the way back to the bed where she lay, limp but still needing more. "I want you," she said, her voice breathy, her lungs relearning how to breathe.

Decker climbed up beside her and reached into the nightstand, extracting a foil packet.

Roxi leaned up on an elbow and held out her hand. "Could I?"

"Of course." He handed her the packet.

She tore it open and rolled the condom over him, her hands caressing him as she slid down his length. "Thanks."

Decker's bark of laughter made her glance his way.

"What?"

"I'm the one who should be thanking you." He dragged her over him and leaned up to kiss her lips. "You're amazing."

"No, I'm clumsy and awkward at this."

"Darlin', you're a natural." He paused. "And if this is as far as you want to go, I'm okay with it."

With her insides pulsing and her channel slick and ready, Roxi shook her head. "No way. I want the whole shebang."

"Then it's up to you now. You take it as slow or fast as you want."

"Really?" She touched his chest with her fingertips and slid her hand down over his ribs. "I get to call the shots?"

"You bet." He lay back, linking his hands behind his head. "I won't touch you unless you want me to."

"Oh, please. Touch me. But you have to promise not to laugh."

He held up two fingers. "Scout's honor." Then he rested the hand on her hip.

She frowned. "I'm betting you were never a Boy Scout."

He shrugged. "No, but I promise."

Not sure what to do, but knowing she wanted him inside her, and the sooner the better, Roxi straddled him, planting her knees on either side of his waist. His erection bumped against her, and she sucked in a sharp breath.

Decker's smile slipped, his jaw tightening.

"I'm not even sure how to do this." Heat rose in her cheeks and her heart pounded so hard in her chest, she was certain he could hear it. So much for the tough bar owner who could do anything she set her mind to. She had never seduced a man or made love to one on her terms. How did one go about it?

Something of her distress must have shown on her face.

"Let me." Decker's big hands gripped her hips, lifted and positioned her exactly the way she needed to make it work.

She leaned her hands on his chest and eased down on his staff.

He slid inside, his girth stretching her, filling her in a wonderfully sensuous way. The friction set off a whole new wave of sensations and she found herself rising and falling over him, her breasts tight, the nipples drawn into tight little buds, her breath hitching in her lungs. If this was what it felt like to really make love, what had she been waiting for?

Apparently, her steady rocking wasn't fast enough for Decker.

Still holding her hips he helped her, guiding her movements, increasing the speed.

His face tensed, his jaw tightened, and he closed

his eyes, thrusting up into her one last time before he held her still, his cock throbbing against the walls of her channel.

Roxi stared down at his face, a feeling of power and satisfaction swelling her chest. "Was it…"

"Perfect," he said on a sigh, opening his eyes to smile up at her.

She lay down on him, her cheek pressed to his skin. The thudding beats of his heart told her he'd been as excited by their coupling as she was. She smiled and languished in the aftermath of a thorough loving, reluctant to break the connection.

When at last he rolled her over beside him, she snuggled against him. "That was amazing."

"Yes, it was. Now, sleep. After working all day, you need it."

She closed her eyes, her body relaxed, her mind a fuzzy happy place where thirteen-year-old girls being raped didn't exist. This was how sex should be.

"Decker?" she said and stifled a yawn. "Is it always this exhausting?"

He laughed softly. "Not always."

"Hmm." With her eyes still closed, she inhaled the scent of him and the lingering musk of sex. "Decker?"

"Yes, Roxi?" His words stirred the tendrils of hair near her temple.

She smiled. "Next time, you can be on top."

CHAPTER 9

DECKER LAY for a long time with his eyes open, his heartbeat finally slowing to a normal pace. The entire time he'd made love to Roxi, he hadn't thought about Allison. With Roxi asleep against his side, memories surfaced of lying in bed with Allison after making love to her.

The two women were as different as night and day. Allison had been quiet when they'd made love, seeming to tolerate it more than she enjoyed it. Not Roxi. She hadn't held back, moaning and calling out his name in the throes of passion.

With Roxi's naked body pressed against his, Decker reflected on what he'd just done. He'd made love to a woman who'd never experienced real, honest sex before. And he'd done it only days after the anniversary of his wife's death.

His own take on the event was nothing short of

confusion. On the one hand, guilt was something he'd carried for a long time. But how long was long enough? On the other hand, making love to the beautiful, capable and sexy bar owner had been more than he could have asked for. Was he ready to move into another relationship? He wasn't the kind of guy who slept around with any willing female. But sleeping with Roxi couldn't be taken lightly. The woman had been raped as a very young, impressionable teen. The fact she hadn't had sex since said a lot.

And he'd made love to her.

The longer he lay there, the more his mind churned, until he gave up on sleep, slipped his arm from under Roxi's neck and rolled out of bed. He padded barefoot and naked into the living room and stood at the floor-to-ceiling window overlooking the Cape. Wind tossed the trees closest to the cottage, and moonlight was blanketed by dark clouds. He couldn't see the water for the utter darkness surrounding them. A howling wail whistled through the eaves.

Decker switched on the television, muting the sound. He tuned in to the local news channel and was surprised to see the evening weatherman still on duty at a quarter past two in the morning. A red banner scrolled across the bottom of the screen, listing counties in the area under severe storm warnings. Then a flashing banner replaced the storm warnings with the order to evacuate by late the next afternoon.

The national weather radar filled the screen with a huge circular blob of green, yellow, orange and red filling the screen south of Cape Cod. The forecast indicated Hurricane Charlie would take a direct path from the coast of North Carolina up to Massachusetts. Cape Cod stood to take the worst of the storm.

"Holy hell," Decker muttered.

"What's wrong?" a soft, gravelly voice said behind him.

He turned to see Roxi standing in the bedroom doorway, naked, pushing loose, blond curls out of her face.

"Did I wake you?" he asked.

"No. I woke on my own, but the bed was empty. Are you okay?" She left that statement hanging, her head tilted to the side, her glance on him.

He swept his gaze over her perfect curves, from her full, lush breasts to the swell of her hips and down incredibly silky thighs to the tight muscles of her calves. God, she was gorgeous.

Decker's groin tightened. He stood and closed the distance between them. "I'm fine, just couldn't sleep. I guess I was too wound up."

Her brows furrowed. "Wound up in a good way or a bad one?"

"Just wound up."

She glanced over his shoulder at the television screen, her frown deepening. "Is that the weatherman?" Roxi slipped around him and came to stand in front of the screen.

Decker followed, resting his hands on her shoulders, liking how smooth and silky her skin was. "They usually blow the weather out of proportion. Once the hurricane hits land, it dies down."

"But they're issuing an evacuation order for all of Cape Cod, and they want everyone out by nightfall." Roxi shook her head and watched the screen for a moment longer. "I have to go."

Decker gripped her arms and turned her to face him. "You sure you want to leave now? It's really late."

"If we have to evacuate before nightfall, I have a lot to do to get ready." Roxi hurried through the cottage gathering her clothing. Once in the bedroom, she stepped into the cutoffs, hooked her bra in place, pulled the straps over her shoulders and tugged her tank top over her head. She grabbed her deck shoes and stopped in front of Decker. "Thanks for a great evening." Cupping his face with the palm of her hands. "No regrets, all right? I'm sure your wife would have expected you to get on with your life."

Decker sighed. "You're the one I was worried about. I hope I didn't scare you off men."

"On the contrary. I hope you'll be around after

the hurricane. But if you aren't, I'll understand. I don't expect any commitment just because we had sex." Then she leaned up on her toes and pressed her lips to his.

He gathered her in his arms and deepened the kiss, his tongue sweeping past her teeth to slide along hers in a soul-wrenching connection he didn't want to end. When he finally lifted his head, he stared down into her eyes. "I'm walking you home."

"No need. Otis will keep me safe. Besides, you'll want to close your storm shutters and pack up."

"What do you have to accomplish? Maybe I can help," Decker said.

"Frank and I can handle it. You need to get off the peninsula before the traffic comes to a standstill."

"I'm not leaving until you and Otis are on your way."

She slipped her feet into her shoes. "Really, we know the drill. We'll be off before evening."

Rather than argue with her, he opened the door. Otis rushed out and ran down the stairs to the beach. The wind whipped a lounge chair around, the legs scraping across the deck.

"I'm walking you home." Decker held up his hand. "I'm not taking no for an answer."

She frowned and then the lines cleared on her forehead. "Okay. Thanks."

Grabbing a flashlight out of a drawer in the kitchen, Decker followed Roxi out the door, closing it securely behind him. Once out on the beach, they had to lean into the wind to keep from being blown over. Sand blew up in their faces, forcing them to squint.

Decker held Roxi's hand and walked all the way to her place and up the stairs to her apartment over the bar. The building blocked the full force of the wind, giving him a moment to properly kiss her.

He pulled Roxi into his arms and rested his forehead against hers. "I'm glad you came over tonight."

"Me too." She smiled up at him. "You've opened a whole new world for me. I realize I don't have to be afraid to be intimate anymore. I can do it without freaking out."

"You're amazing. And I want to see you again. Maybe this time I can take you out on a real date."

"I'd like that." She touched his cheek with her fingers. "Be careful leaving the Cape."

"I will." He didn't add that he'd be careful to leave with her, and not any sooner.

Otis bumped into the backs of his legs.

Decker laughed. "I think someone wants in the apartment."

Roxi unlocked her door and let Otis in, then stepped inside, turning to face Decker as she closed the door.

He waited until he heard the lock click in place before he descended the stairs to the beach. His walk back to his cottage was quick with the wind behind him. He let himself in and glanced around at the contents of the little house. He didn't have much to pack. A suitcase of clothing, his laptop and files were all he would take.

By the time daylight arrived, gray and cloudy, he had everything he needed sitting by the door and all the storm shutters pulled in and latched securely. He wanted to check on Hank's place and make sure all the storm shutters were in place before he headed over to the bar to assist Roxi and Frank with their efforts. If they had to board the windows, they'd need help. The wind was almost too strong to allow them to position sheets of plywood over the windows.

Decker drove around to the secluded beach cottage Hank used when he was at the cape. He found the key Hank had hidden beneath a flower pot on the front deck and went from room to room on the inside, making certain everything was shut down, locked up and put away. Hank had stored all the outside patio furniture in a shed before he'd left and closed the storm shutters. The cottage was ready for the coming storm.

By the time Decker drove the short distance through town to the Gone Fishin' Bar & Grill, the residents of the little town were up and moving, packing their vehicles with their belongings and closing shutters. The business owners hung large sheets of plywood in their windows, boarding up in case the winds sent objects flying through the air.

Outside the Bar & Grill, Frank, Saul and Roxi struggled to get a sheet of plywood in place, the wind wreaking havoc with their efforts.

Decker parked his SUV and climbed out. Otis ran to greet him. His tail wagged and he nuzzled Decker's hand. "Hey, Otis. Are you helping Roxi hang plywood?"

The dog pressed his nose into Decker's palm, then turned to lope back toward the bar as if saying *follow me*.

"You're just in time," Frank called out. "We've been working at this since first light, but it's only getting harder."

"I can do this," Roxi insisted.

"Maybe you can, but I can't," Frank said.

"I'm here, you might as well let me help." Decker grabbed the corner of the heavy plywood from Roxi's hands.

Frank winked at her. "He's a keeper."

She frowned and grumbled, "I could have done it myself."

"I know." Decker nodded, his lips curling into a gentle smile. "But there are a lot of sheets to do and if we want to get off the peninsula before dark, we'd better get cracking."

With a nod, she stepped back. "Saul and I will start moving the outside tables and chairs inside."

The four of them worked all day, with the weather getting worse each passing hour.

A line of cars with the residual vacationers and locals formed on the road, headed inland. Still, the team worked, boarding, storing and locking things down to keep them from being carried off by what Frank called *a brisk ocean breeze*.

Once the boards were all in place and the outside furniture had been stowed, Roxi turned to Frank. "Do you need help at your place?"

"No. I closed it up before I came over here, and my vehicle is packed to the gills."

"Good." Roxi tilted her head toward Frank's vehicle. "Take Saul and get going. At least the line of cars has thinned."

Frank shook his head. "I'm not leaving without you."

She hugged the older man. "I'll be fine. Decker will make sure I get out on time." She turned to him and grinned. "Won't you?"

Roxi's smile nearly floored Decker. He'd never seen this side of her. The more dangerous the situation, the more she threw herself at the work involved, and the more animated she became. The woman obviously loved a challenge, and Mother Nature was sending one her way. With the wind whipping her hair around her face and not a stitch of make up on, Roxi looked happier, more alive and beautiful than ever.

Decker's heart squeezed tightly, and he found himself falling even deeper for this incredible woman.

"I'll make sure she's safe," he promised. He dragged his gaze from Roxi and shook the older man's hand. "Go. We'll be right behind you."

Frank frowned at Roxi. "I'm counting on it."

Roxi and Decker watched as Frank and Saul climbed into Frank's vehicle and slid into the slowly moving traffic.

"What's left?" Decker asked.

"I have a couple boxes I need to carry out to my car, and I'll be ready."

"Good, because the sun is setting, and those clouds looked downright wicked." Decker pointed to the wall of black clouds roiling in the sky, headed straight for them.

Roxi led the way up the stairs to her small apartment, grabbed a box and passed Decker. She nodded to another box on the floor. "I've got this one, if you can get that one."

"Got it." Decker lifted the box and carried it down the stairs behind Roxi.

She loaded the boxes into the trunk and hurried back up the stairs without saying a word to him.

Not that Decker expected anything, but now that they were alone, without Frank's eagle eye watching over them, he'd expected her to say something about their night together.

Back in her apartment, Roxi was rolling a suitcase toward the door. "If you can take this one down, I'll lock up."

He took the case from her and set it aside. Then he took her hand in his, pulled her against him and kissed her long and hard.

When he let go of her, she stepped backward, her eyes wide. She pushed her hair back from her face and slid a tongue across her lips. "What was that for?"

"I'm sorry. I just couldn't resist."

She glanced down at her dirty shorts and shirt and tried to shove her wild hair behind her ears. "I'm a mess."

"The prettiest mess around." He turned her and swatted her bottom. "Now lock up. I made a promise to Frank that I'd get you out of here on time, and I don't want to disappoint the man. He looks like he could whoop my ass with one hand tied behind his back."

Roxi took one step, spun back around, planted a kiss on his lips and hurried back through the apartment, making one last pass.

"What was that for?" he called out to her back.

"Just because," she said over her shoulder. "Chop, chop. We have to leave before dark. The weatherman said the hurricane will make landfall around midnight, but the storm surge and winds will be pretty bad ahead of it."

For a moment, Decker considered following Roxi into her bedroom and taking her there on her floral-patterned comforter. But one glance out the window reminded him of the limited time they had left before they needed to be off the peninsula. He forced himself to snatch up the suitcase and carry it down to her waiting Toyota RAV4. She already had several boxes jammed into the back. How she'd get the rest of her things into the limited space was a mystery to Decker. Shifting the contents, he made a hole large enough for the suitcase and shoved it in.

When he climbed back up the stairs, he found Roxi standing in the middle of the living room, a bulging suitcase standing beside her. "I missed this one, but I think I now have everything I can't live without. The rest will just have to weather the storm. Oh, wait. I almost forgot Mom." She crossed to a shelf in the corner of the living room and lifted a photograph of a woman with a striking resemblance to Roxi. She had the same blond hair and blue eyes, with a few more crow's feet on the corners. She definitely had the same smile.

"This is your mother?" Decker glanced down at the photograph. "You look just like her."

Roxi shook her head. "Mom was much prettier. Inside and out. She carried the load for so many years as a single mother trying to raise a kid. I wish

I could have helped her more." She unzipped the suitcase and packed the photo beneath several layers of soft cotton shirts. Then she zipped the suitcase and straightened. "I'm ready."

"Good. It's getting dark out there." Decker would have preferred leaving when Frank had but hadn't thought a few minutes would make that big of a difference, until he stepped outside. The clouds had thickened and churned, racing across the sky. Lightning flickered, and thunder rumbled close behind. "We need to go."

"Agreed." With her hand on the door knob, ready to pull it closed, Roxi glanced around the small room. "Where's Otis?"

CHAPTER 10

A BRIGHT FLASH of lightning blinded Roxi as she glanced down the stairs. Not even a second later, thunder boomed so loud, it made her jump.

As protective as Otis was, he was a big scaredy-cat when it came to thunderstorms.

Decker stuck his head inside the apartment and called out, "Otis, come!"

Nothing moved.

Roxi shoved the suitcase toward Decker. "You carry this down, I'll check under the bed."

Decker laughed. "Under the bed?"

Roxi gave Decker a stern look. "Don't judge." Her lips twitched. "Otis is a big baby when it comes to storms."

Decker went down the stairs while Roxi reentered the apartment and searched every nook and cranny, which didn't take long in the small space.

Worry settled in the middle of her chest.

Decker arrived at the top of the stairs as Roxi pulled the door close. "He's not in the apartment."

"Could Frank have taken him?"

"Not a chance." Roxi shook her head. "Frank barely had room for himself and Saul."

"Could he be in the bar?"

"Maybe." She pulled her keys to the bar out of her purse, descended the stairs and unlocked the door to the kitchen.

"I'll make a pass around the building while you check inside." Decker headed around the side of the building.

Roxi entered the kitchen, flipped on the light and checked under every counter, behind the empty trash cans and stacked boxes. "Otis!" she called out, moving into the main room. The German shepherd wasn't behind the bar. After a thorough pass through the large seating area with the chairs stacked neatly on the tables and the outside tables and chairs pushed up against the walls, Roxi was no closer to finding Otis.

"He wasn't outside hiding in the bushes," Decker's voice called out from behind the bar.

"I have no idea where he could have gone." More worried than she cared to admit, Roxi led the way out of the bar and locked the door behind Decker, making a decision as she did. Grabbing her hair and holding it away from her face, she peered up at Decker in the light from the back porch of the bar. "Look, you need to go while you still can," she said, shouting over the wail of the wind. "The tide is already rising. If the storm surge gets much higher, we could be cut off from the mainland. You should go while the going's good."

Decker's bark of laughter startled Roxi. "You don't really think I'd leave without you."

"You should. I have no idea how long it will take to find Otis, and the weather is bad enough and will only get worse."

As if to emphasize her point, a cardboard box bounced past them and continued rolling down the nearly empty street. The traffic had thinned to the last few residents heading to the mainland.

"I'm not leaving without you," Decker said.

"And I'm not leaving without Otis."

"Then let's find him." Decker stepped away from the building and shined his light past the end of the bar toward the water. Waves crashed against the shore and peer. "Does Otis ever visit other houses?"

Roxi shook her head. "Only Frank's when I have to go to the mainland without him. But that's two miles away and I never walked him there. He always rides in the car. The only other house he's been in is yours." She looked up at Decker, her brows dipping. "You don't think he went back to your house, do you?"

"If there's any possibility he went there, we'd better check it out."

Roxi started for the beach, but Decker caught her arm.

"The surge has pushed into the shoreline and it's getting too rough near the water. We'll take my SUV and drive around." He slipped his arm around Roxi's waist and, shielding her from the worst of the wind, led the way to his vehicle, shining the light in front of them.

Roxi prayed Otis hadn't gone down to the water. The way the surf pounded the beach, he could have been swept away. No matter how good of a swimmer he was, the tide would win the battle.

She scanned the sides of the road on the short ride to Decker's cottage but didn't see any sign of Otis. Rain started falling as they climbed out of his car and ran for the house.

"Otis!"

Lightning flashed, piercing the pelting rain. Thunder followed immediately behind. Bolt after bolt of electricity shimmered across the sky illuminating the billowing clouds.

"Otis!" Roxi called out, the sound of her voice whipped away by the wind. If not for Decker's steadying arm around her, she'd have been blown over.

With the flashlight beam barely shining bright enough to see into the shadows, and rain driving into them like a power-washer's spray, they circled the cottage, checking behind bushes and shining the light beneath the tall peers supporting the house and the deck above. Just when Roxi thought they'd failed in finding the missing dog, the flash-light's beam glinted off two red orbs.

"Wait!" Roxi grabbed Decker's hand with the flashlight and shined it toward the farthest corner beneath the house. There in the shadows crouched Otis, his entire body trembling with each boom of thunder.

"Otis!" Roxi cried and, ducking low, she eased beneath the house to where the dog hid. "Oh, baby, come with me. We'll take care of you."

Otis dug his feet into the dirt and refused to come out of his hiding place.

Decker hunkered low and eased up beside Roxi. "Hold this." He handed her the flashlight, grabbed the dog's collar and pulled him into his arms. Then he lifted Otis and carried him out into the open.

By then, the sky had opened up and sheets of rain, carried on the wind pummeled them.

Roxi couldn't see past the end of her arm and the blasting wind nearly pushed her over. But what scared her more was when she swept the flashlight beam toward the Cape, she could see that the tide was near where they stood. The storm surge had arrived.

"We have to get to high ground," Decker shouted over the wind.

A sheet of metal roofing peeled off the home next to Decker's and flew toward them.

Roxi screamed and ducked.

Decker, still holding Otis, turned and ducked, but not enough. The metal glanced off his back, hit his head and continued on.

Decker dropped to his knees, his hold on Otis intact.

Roxi realized they were too late to get off the peninsula. With the wind flinging debris everywhere and the tide rising at an alarming rate, they didn't stand a chance. "Give me the key to your cottage," she shouted.

"It's in my pocket," he said, swaying, where he knelt.

With water streaming down her face, she reached into Decker's pocket and found his keys. She helped him to his feet and up the flight of stairs to the top. When she fit the one that looked like a house key into the lock, she almost cried with relief. The lock turned, the door swung open and they scrambled inside.

Roxi turned and leaned hard on the door to close it against the elements. The storm raged around the house as if angry they had dared to shelter inside.

Decker set Otis on the floor. The dog promptly

shook, showering Decker and the floor around him with droplets of water.

"I'll get a towel." Roxi headed for the small bathroom off the bedroom where she had made love to Decker the night before. After all that had happened, it seemed so long ago. As she passed the bed, her heartbeat fluttered, and her body warmed with the memory.

Focusing on the wet dog and the injured man, she hurried through the bedroom, grabbed a towel and a couple of washcloths from the linen closet and hurried back to the living area.

The windows were shuttered against the storm making the cottage feel more like a cave or cocoon, closed off and protected.

Roxi chose not to dwell on the fact hurricane winds could level every building in its path, downing trees and pushing massive ships aground. Even if the cottage survived the hurricane-force winds, the debris or entire boats and ships in its path could be shoved into the pilings, sending the cottage crashing into the storm surge.

She forced the negative thoughts from her head and tossed the towel over Otis. To Decker, she said, "Sit."

He collapsed on the couch and touched the back of his head. When he brought his hand around to look at it, it was covered in bright red blood.

Roxi pressed one of the cloths to the back of his

head where blood matted his hair. "Hold this and apply pressure."

While he did as she said, Roxi wet the other cloth in the kitchen sink and hurried back to him.

Decker turned sideways to allow her to sit on the couch behind him.

Carefully dabbing at the blood, Roxy located the injury. "It's just a little cut, but it comes complete with a goose egg knot. Good news is that the bleeding has just about stopped."

"Good. I want to get a shower before the electricity goes off." He pushed to his feet and turned to her. His dark brows waggled. "The shower is big enough for two, if you'd care to join me."

Roxi laughed, her pulse ratcheted up to full speed. "With a hurricane crashing in around us, you want to take a shower with me?"

"Damn right. If we're wiped off the face of the planet by this storm, I want to die making love to a beautiful woman." He held out his hand for hers. "Are you with me?"

"That's some invitation, slugger." Roxi stood, her heartrate already elevated by danger, her pulse increasing with the amount of passion reflected in Decker's eyes. "Are you sure you're up to it? You've had a head injury."

"All the more reason to throw caution to the wind." Decker's gaze locked with hers, his voice rich, his tone deep with emotion. "I've spent the last two years of my life wishing I was dead. Now that I want to live, I want every day, hour and minute to count."

Roxi laid her hand in his. "And I've spent the past fourteen years afraid to live my life to the fullest, hiding away from the world by staying here on the Cape. If you hadn't come along, I would still be living only half of a life." She slapped her hand in his and laughed. "I'm in!"

They ran for the bathroom, clothes flying in their wake

Otis crouched beneath the dining table.

Roxi had never made love in the shower, but under Decker's tutelage, she learned it could be every bit as sexy as in a bed, albeit a little more challenging. They laughed and soaped each other's bodies as the storm raged outside, shaking the walls of the cottage. Roxi touched Decker all over and he reciprocated, stroking her in her most sensitive place, making her blood sing and her insides burn.

He brought her to the edge and launched her over, her cries echoing off the tiles.

When she could form a coherent thought again, she pressed her palms to his face. "You make me feel so…so…uninhibited." Though she'd already come, and her legs were like wet noodles, she wouldn't feel complete until Decker filled her. She looked him in the eye and whispered, "As crazy as the storm is outside, I'm on fire inside, and I want you."

Decker scooped her up by the backs of her thighs, wrapped her legs around his waist and stepped out of the shower. Dripping wet, he headed for the door, his face set.

"Was it something I said?" Roxi snagged a towel from a bar on their way out of the bathroom.

"Most definitely." Decker winked, a wicked gleam in his eyes. "The protection is in the other room."

"Oh." Her core tightened, and she eased down to his erection, teasing him with her wet entrance. "You sure you can wait that long?"

"No, I'm not sure at all."

Roxi's stomach fluttered at the intensity of his confession. She held on as he carried her into the bedroom. "Shouldn't we dry off first?"

"Details, details." He sighed and set her on her feet. Then he took the towel from her hands and patted her dry from the top of her head to the tips of her toes, taking an inordinate and knee-melting amount of time at her breasts and the juncture of her thighs. By the time she dried him off, she wasn't sure she could wait another minute. She hopped onto the bed and smiled as the storm pounded the house and Otis crept beneath the bed.

CHAPTER 11

DECKER STOOD FOR A MOMENT, drinking in the sight of Roxi, lying across the comforter, naked, a smile curving her full, lush lips, her eyes sparkling. She wanted him. And by all that was crazy, he wanted her too. They could be washed away by the hurricane at any moment, but he knew in his heart, he'd die a happy man as long as he had this time with Roxi.

The woman was strong and worldly in so many ways, and just as eagerly inexperienced in others. He worried that he was pushing her too fast, but she seemed happy to let him touch her and bring out the sex-starved woman in her.

She stared up at him, her blue-eyed gaze intense, penetrating. "Remember," she said. "This time, you're on top." Color rose in her cheeks even as her knees fell to the side, and she spread her legs, inviting him in.

Holy hell. He couldn't resist. Decker dove into the nightstand for a condom, ripped it open and rolled it over himself, then he climbed onto the bed like a conquering hero, claiming his prize. Taking deep, steadying breaths, he had to remind himself to move slowly, not to scare her or set off any residual memories.

God, he wished he could find the bastard that raped the thirteen-year-old Roxi. He'd kill him and leave him for the buzzards to pick clean.

Roxi slid her hands over his chest and locked them behind his head, careful not to touch the lump he'd sustained in the storm.

Strong, sexy Roxi, who'd chosen to let him be the one to show her how loving should be done. His heart swelled.

The woman beneath him slid her hands back over his chest and lower to grip his hips. "I want you. Now." She increased the pressure, pulling him toward her.

Decker slid into her, all the way until he could go no farther. This was where he wanted to be. This woman made him feel more alive than he had in a very long time and he wanted to keep on living if only to be with her.

THEY MADE LOVE, holding and caressing each other until the electricity blinked out around midnight. It didn't matter to Decker. He didn't need a light to know where she was. When they were completely satiated, they slept, curled inside each other's arms.

Decker slept deeper than he'd done since the accident, no dreams to wake him, only the sound of Roxi's soft breathing to lull him into a happy place. When he woke it was to the soft gray of dawn, edging past the cracks between the storm shutter slats.

Otis stood beside the bed and woofed.

Roxi stirred and stretched, her arm sliding across Decker's chest. "He needs to go outside."

"I'll take him." Decker pushed the sheet aside and flicked the switch on the lamp on the nightstand. Nothing happened. "Electricity is still off."

"It will probably be off for a couple of days," Roxi said, her voice gravelly with sleep.

Decker found a pair of shorts in one of his drawers and pulled them on.

Otis trotted across the wooden floor, toenails clicking, headed for the door to the deck.

With all the windows covered, Decker didn't know what to expect outside. By the silence, he'd guess the storm had passed.

When he opened the door, Otis ran out on the deck and down to the beach. Debris had washed up on the sand, including a fishing boat, boards from what might once have been someone's dock and other items. It was a mess, but nothing that couldn't be cleaned up in time for next summer's tourists.

Otis took care of business and returned to the cottage, lying down on the rug in the living room.

Eager to get back to Roxi, Decker hurried to the bedroom. Roxi sat propped against the headboard, the sheet pulled up over her breasts.

Decker's cock twitched in his shorts, hardening as he took in the way her blond hair tumbled about her shoulders, brushing the swells of her breasts.

Roxi stared at him across the room and slowly lowered the sheet, exposing her chest.

The shorts couldn't come off fast enough and Decker dove for the bed.

Roxi chuckled and threw back the sheet, rolling into his arms. They made love, taking their time, exploring each other's bodies.

When at last they lay back, Decker nuzzled Roxi's neck. "You know we could be stuck here for days."

"Mmm," she murmured. "And that's a bad thing?"

"Not at all." He slid his hand down to one of her nipples and teased it into a tight little bud. "I like having you all to myself."

"Greedy much?" Roxi wove her fingers through the hairs on his chest.

"Where you're concerned, hell yeah."

"What happens when everything returns to the way it was? What then?" she asked.

"Frankly, I don't think it ever will." He moved his hand to her other nipple, stroking it and tweaking until it budded into a tight little knot. "I don't know what's happening between us, but I don't want it to stop."

"Me either." Roxi cupped her hand over his on her breast. "I like this…what you do to me…how you make me feel."

"And I like the way you feel in my arms." He stared into her eyes. "Is it love?" He shrugged. "If it isn't yet, it soon will be. Are you willing to give it a shot?" Decker held his breath, waiting for her response.

Gone was his reluctance to move on with his life, his survivor's guilt fading in the light of the sun after the storm. He wanted this chance to get to know Roxi better, and maybe fall in love again. For the first time since Allison's death, he believed in the possibility.

Roxi snuggled closer, resting her cheek against his chest a smile curling her lips. "I've never been in love, but if it's anywhere near as intense as I feel when I'm with you…I want to give it a chance." She pushed up on one elbow and stared down into his eyes. "Count me in." Then she kissed him, and Decker held on with both hands.

EPILOGUE

"HEY, HANK, YOU GOT A MINUTE?" Decker rested his foot on the deck railing and pressed his cell phone to his ear.

"For you, Decker, I have all the minutes you want," Hank Patterson said into Decker's ear.

"About that job you talked about with the Brotherhood Protectors..."

"What about it?" Hank asked.

"Any possibility you could use a guy who bases off the east coast?" Decker asked. He looked out over the calm waters. He'd spent the week cleaning up the beach front outside his cottage and making repairs to the Gone Fishin' Bar and Grill with Roxi. Now that he had a minute to spare, he'd decided to get on with the rest of his life, doing what he did best.

"I hadn't considered setting up an office on the

east coast, but I have had inquiries about providing protective services for big shots with money out there. Are you telling me you want to be a Brotherhood Protector?"

Decker nodded, though he knew Hank couldn't see him. "I am. With the tourist season dying down, odd jobs on the Cape will be few and far between."

"Why don't you come out to Montana? I have plenty of work out here."

In the distance, Roxi and Otis walked along the sand, on their way back from a walk.

Decker's chest swelled with all the love he felt for the woman. "No, I need to be able to come home to Cape Cod. Montana would be a little too far for that. It's okay if you don't think it will work out."

"No, no. Wait. I think it's a great idea. I could use someone I trust out there to set up shop. I gotta tell you, I was approached while Sadie and I were on the Cape to provide services for the area and parts of Massachusetts and Connecticut. I didn't seriously consider it because it was so far from Montana, but with you there, I don't see why we can't set up an east coast office."

"I'd be glad to head it up, or even just be one of your agents. I just need to get back to work before I get too rusty to be of any good."

Hank snorted. "I'm not buying that. You know the saying, *Once a SEAL, always a SEAL.*"

"Goes right along with the other one *The only easy day was yesterday.*"

A chuckle filled Decker's ear.

"That about sums up the life of a Brotherhood Protector, as well." Hank paused. "You sure you want to do this? I can't guarantee a cake walk."

"I don't like cake. I just want to be able to get home often enough to have a life."

"Decker, I'm glad to hear it," Hank said softly. "Allison would have wanted you to move on. I take it you have?"

Again, Decker nodded and smiled at Roxi as she and Otis climbed the steps to the deck. "I have my memories. I'll never forget her."

Roxi wrapped her arms around his waist and whispered in his free ear. "And I wouldn't want you to."

"She must be special," Hank said.

"You have no idea just how special." Decker pressed a kiss to Roxi's forehead and then one to her lips. "I've gotta go. I left something burning on the stove."

Hank laughed. "I get it. She's there with you, right?"

Roxi leaned close and spoke into the phone, "Yes, sir, I am. Hi, Hank, Roxi here."

"Holy hell, Roxi?" Hank's bark of laughter sounded in Decker's ear. "Should have known by the way you looked at her every time you ordered another drink." A sound in the background on the other end of the line made Hank pause. "Sadie said hello."

"As I was saying," Decker took control of the phone. "I left something burning. I'm in. We can nail down the details later." He clicked the off button and tossed the phone onto a chair cushion.

Roxi tipped back her head and smiled up at him. "What did you leave burning?"

He stared down into her eyes, his love for this woman threatening to overwhelm him. "You, baby. You're the fire I left burning."

"What are you going to do about it?"

"I sure as hell am not going to put it out." He bent and scooped her up into his arms.

"Glad to hear it. I was thinking we might want to stoke the flames."

"I couldn't agree with you more." Decker kissed her lips and carried her into the cottage. "I'm sure glad you saved my life that night on the beach."

"I saved your life?" She shook her head. "If you hadn't come back for me, I'd have drowned in that riptide."

"I guess we saved each other," he settled her on the couch, too turned on by her to make it all the way to the bedroom.

"Did you get the job?" she asked.

"I did."

"In Montana?" She leaned up on her elbows.

"Because if you go to Montana, I'll have to follow you. You're not leaving me behind."

"You'd go with me to Montana?" Decker raised his eyebrows. "I thought you never wanted to leave the Cape."

"I don't. But I kind of like you. If staying with you meant going to Montana, I'd do it." Her gaze dropped. "If you wanted me to come, that is."

He chuckled. "Oh, babe, I'd want you to come." He pulled her into his arms. "But you're not going to Montana."

"I'm not?" Her gaze shot back to his, a frown pulling her eyebrows together. "You don't want me to come?"

"No." He shook his head. "I want you to stay."

"But I don't want to stay without you."

"What if you stayed with me?"

Her frown deepened. "What do you mean? You did get the job, didn't you?"

He nodded. "I did." Then he grinned. "But I'm setting up the east coast office of Brotherhood Protectors. And I'm thinking it will base out of the Cape." He kissed the tip of her nose. "Sweetheart, you're stuck with me."

She flung her arms around his neck and let out a little squeal.

Then they were kissing, shedding clothing and rolling into the sheets.

Otis woofed his own excitement and then settled on the floor as Decker made love to Roxi.

A cool breeze lifted the curtains at the open window, but Decker didn't notice. The heat he and Roxi generated promised to burn well into the night.

He'd found his home in Cape Cod with a woman he could make new memories with and he had a job that fit his skillset.

Life was good, and he didn't want to waste a minute of it.

THE BILLIONAIRE HUSBAND TEST

BILLIONAIRE ONLINE DATING SERVICE
SERIES BOOK #1

New York Times & USA Today
Bestselling Author

ELLE JAMES

CHAPTER 1

"DON'T LEAVE LOVE up to luck. With the help of my firm and heavily tested computer algorithms, you will have a ninety-nine point nine percent chance of finding your perfect match." The attractive young woman, wearing a soft gray business suit and standing in front of the white board, clicked a hand-held remote control. A picture of a couple embracing at sunset on a beach materialized on the white surface. "What do you think? Willing to give my program a shot?"

"I don't know." Frank Cooper Johnson sat at the conference table with the other members of the Billionaires Anonymous Club. "Am I the only one who thinks this is a bad idea?"

"Mr. Johnson—" Leslie Lamb began.

"Call him Coop. All his friends call him that." Maxwell Smithson grinned.

"For the sake of argument, give my friend Leslie the benefit of the doubt." Taggert Bronson rose to stand beside the presenter. "Think about it. Didn't we all make the same plans? Work hard, work smart, make our first million by thirty, start a family by thirty-five...We're all on track—only better–instead of millions, we made our billions by thirty." Tag pointed to Gage Tate. "How's that media empire going?" He nodded toward Sean O'Leary. "Your oil speculating has you sitting pretty, doesn't it, Sean? And Coop, you and I are making billions on our financial investments. Have any of you even thought about the next step in our plan? How many of you are even dating?"

Sean raised his hand. "I've been dating."

"The same girl more than once?" Tag asked.

"Using a computer to find a mate just doesn't seem right." Coop pushed back his chair and rose. "When I find the woman I want to marry, I'll do it the old-fashioned way."

Tag snorted. "And meet her at a bar?"

"Any of you have any luck lately going to a bar and not being slammed by the paparazzi?"

Gage sighed. "Though I hate to admit it, the man has a point. I can't step outside my condo without being hit by at least a dozen cameras, much less go to dinner with anyone without being bombarded."

Leslie smiled. "That's the beauty of BODS—"

"Seriously?" Sean shook his head. "BODS?"

The woman drew herself up to her full five-foot-three inches and stared down her nose at Sean. "Billionaire Online Dating Service—BODS. It's an acronym, so sue me. As I was saying, the beauty of the system is that the communication is all done anonymously. You meet real woman, not money-grubbing, limelight-seeking gold-diggers."

Gage frowned. "They won't know that we're loaded?"

"Financial status is not one of the questions we ask on the online data collection system. I perform a background check on each entrant and the computer does the matching."

Tag spread his hands. "Don't you love it? And the match is all based on your own personality profile." He dropped his hands when none of the others spoke. "What have you got to lose?"

Shaking his head, Coop grumbled, "Our dignity. Participation is admitting we're hopeless at finding a date."

Leslie shook her head. "Not at all. The program gives you a better chance of finding someone who truly fits the life-style of your dreams. Tell you what. As my first customers—"

Gage shot to his feet. "Whoa, wait a minute. First?" He stared across at Tag. "I thought you said this system was proven?"

"It is…on volunteers." Tag held up his hands.

"Leslie hasn't yet charged for her services. Calm down."

Coop crossed his arms, ready for the meeting to be over. "I don't relish being someone's guinea pig."

"You aren't." Leslie sucked in a deep breath and let it out. "Tell you what, how about I let you use my service free? If you find the woman of your dreams, then you pay me what you think the experience was worth."

"Can't get fairer than that." Tag grinned. "Who wants to be first to sign up?"

"I think you should be." Cooper pinned Tag with a challenging stare.

"I'm already in the system and aiming for a date next Friday." Tag's eyes narrowed. "How about it, Coop? Or are you afraid?"

Hell yeah, Cooper was afraid. What kind of loser would the computer match him up with? Then again, he wouldn't admit to any of them that the idea of dating was worse than public speaking...and he hated public speaking. That's why he worked the financial market and stayed behind the scenes. He lived on his ranch, raised his horses quietly—no fanfare and no paparazzi as long as he didn't step out on a date. So far, the arrangement had been very lucrative with no distractions. Lonely, but lucrative, about summed up his life.

"Look, Leslie is in a situation no different than we were when we started out." Tag continued,

"Give her business a chance. One date. That's all she's asking."

"Fine," Cooper said. "Anything to get this meeting over with."

Leslie's face bloomed with a huge smile. "I'll take you in Tag's office, one at a time to enter your data and show you the ropes. The process won't take long and you'll have your match. You won't regret your decision. I promise."

Cooper was already regretting his agreement, and he hadn't even been matched yet.

EMMA JACOB'S cell phone vibrated, indicating a text message. Sitting at a stoplight, she glanced at the message and sighed.

Set an extra plate at dinner. The message was from her oldest brother, Ace. More than likely, the guest was another attempt at fixing her up with a man. For the past month, all four of her brothers had taken it upon themselves to find Emma a husband.

Great, that's all she needed, more husband candidates forced on her by the worst match-makers ever in Jacobs family history. Granted, her four brothers meant well, but really? If she'd wanted another man in her life, she'd have gone out and chosen one herself.

Truth was she was happy just the way things were. Well, almost. She'd have been much happier if the love of her life had lived long enough for them to be married, have children and grow old together. But that hadn't been in the cards. Not once Marcus was deployed, got hit by an improvised explosion device and died before being transported back to the states.

Her throat tightened and she twisted the diamond engagement ring on her finger. For two years, she'd been mourning his death. You'd think her brothers would let it be, instead of telling her she should get back in the saddle.

Emma slipped the ring from her finger and tucked it into her wallet. Maybe removing the ring would lead her brothers to think she was ready to move on, even if she wasn't. That and her trip to Dallas and a meeting with the one friend, Leslie Lamb, she'd made in her grieving group would set her plan in motion. Emma had a special favor to ask of her friend. One she hoped would solve all her problems with her brothers.

"You want what?" Leslie leaned across her desk an hour later, tapping her pen against the notepad she'd been scribbling on.

"I want you to set me up on a date with a man that will completely fail to impress my brothers." Emma ticked off on her fingers. "He has to be nice looking. That fact will throw off the boys.

Preferably someone who makes his living sitting behind a desk." She'd pictured a pasty computer geek, but didn't want to be that crude in front of Leslie.

"Let me get this straight. You want this date to fail?" Leslie shook her head. "I'm building a business, not tearing it down. How will that look to the guy I'm setting you up with if I match him with someone totally wrong for his preferences?"

Emma sat back, frowning. "Hmm, sorry. That's pretty narrow-minded, thinking only of myself." She chewed on her lip for a moment. "I guess I could go find some other online dating service and play Russian roulette." She sat up. "I'm sorry, Leslie, the idea was stupid. Just forget I asked. I know how hard you've worked to put together the business plan and line up investors for your dating service. I wish you lots of luck." Emma gathered her purse and stood. "I have to get back to the ranch before feeding time."

"Wait." Leslie left her chair and rounded her desk, laying a hand on Emma's arm. "Do me a favor first and fill out a form on my computer. Be honest, don't fudge the data and let's see what happens."

Already shaking her head, Emma backed toward the door. "I don't want to set you up for failure. I'm really not interested in finding love. I had it."

Leslie squeezed her arm. "I know. Thinking of

loving anyone else is hard, isn't it? I know exactly where you are. I haven't even tried, yet."

"Yet. At least you might some day." Emma shook her head, pain pinching her throat. "Not me. I had the love of my life. I don't want second best."

"At least, give the system a chance to find a match that closely suits you. Give him one date, and maybe your brothers will get off your back."

"I don't know. I don't like leading someone on when I don't want it to go anywhere."

"Just do it and keep an open mind. We screen our clients and do background checks. At least, you know you won't be getting an ex-con or child molester. You won't regret it, I promise."

Emma chewed on her lip. Leslie's proposal might do the trick. She just didn't want her friend's matchmaking business to suffer the consequences. "The date is doomed to failure. Are you sure you want to take the hit?"

"Be honest with the data. The system will do the rest and I'm willing to take the risk."

For a long moment, Emma stared into her friend's hopeful face. "Anyone ever tell you saying no to you is hard?" She laughed. "If you keep that up, you should get lots of business."

Leslie nodded, a smug smile on her lips. "I plan on it. I only want others to have a chance at the love you and I have both known. I wouldn't have missed the experience for the world."

Emma sighed. "Me either." She let Leslie lead her into a spare office where she could use the computer to enter her data. Emma made a point of putting it all out there—the good, the bad and the not so attractive. If the system found someone to date her, the result would be a miracle. And once out at the ranch with her brothers running him through his paces, any prospect would soon learn no one would equal their expectations.

She'd be off the hook and free to pursue her own goals and dreams. Which included purchasing Old Man Rausch's one-hundred-and-fifty-acre spread on Willow Creek. The place would be all hers, paid for with the money she'd been saving from her work as a horse trainer for the T-Bar-M Ranch. Once she lived on her own, her brothers couldn't interfere with her life.

A good plan, and one she intended to see through.

As she stepped into her truck to make the long drive back to the Rockin' J Ranch, a cool breeze swept across the parking lot, lifting the hair off the back of her neck, surrounding her like a caress. She glanced at the sky. No clouds. Weird. The temperature read-out on the bank sign on the corner listed ninety-nine degrees. Heat waves rippled upward from the black pavement, and Emma had yet to switch on the truck AC. So where had the cool breeze come from? She could swear she smelled a faint hint of musky aftershave, the kind Marcus liked to wear when they'd gone out on dates.

Emma's chest tightened and she sat still, trying to recapture the scent. Finally, she gave up. She had to be imagining the smell. All this talk with Leslie about having loved the man of their dreams had played havoc with her memories. Nothing a good round of stall mucking wouldn't cure.

She'd never told anyone she thought Marcus's spirit lingered around her, keeping her company when she was lonely or afraid. Her brothers would have her in a shrink's office quicker than she could say *lickety-split*. At night, when she lay in bed, missing him so badly it hurt, a light breeze would stir the curtains and waft around her. She'd stare at the picture of them laughing on the beach at South Padre Island and sigh. Marcus was everything she'd ever wanted in life. With him gone, she didn't have anything to aim for, except the ranch and her independence.

If her plan to bring a "date" home to her brothers worked, she'd be one step closer to that independence she so craved and to quelling her brothers' determination to marry her off. The ball was in Leslie's court to find the right man to pull off the plan.

"Please be everything I asked for," Emma whispered as she cranked the truck engine. Another gentle breeze blew in through the open window and trailed across her skin, lifting more goose bumps. She shrugged and shifted into drive. Emma chastised herself for her morbid thoughts. If she didn't stop thinking every peculiar thing that happened in her life was a sign, she'd be forced to commit herself to the nearest psychiatric ward for evaluation.

The Billionaire Husband Test (#1)

ABOUT THE AUTHOR

ELLE JAMES also writing as MYLA JACKSON is a *New York Times* and *USA Today* Bestselling author of books including cowboys, intrigues and paranormal adventures that keep her readers on the edges of their seats. With over eighty works in a variety of sub-genres and lengths she has published with Harlequin, Samhain, Ellora's Cave, Kensington, Cleis Press, and Avon. When she's not at her computer, she's traveling, snow skiing, boating, or riding her ATV, dreaming up new stories. Learn more about Elle James at www.ellejames.com

Website | Facebook | Twitter | GoodReads | Newsletter | BookBub | Amazon

Or visit her alter ego Myla Jackson at mylajackson.com
Website | Facebook | Twitter | Newsletter

Follow Me!
www.ellejames.com
ellejames@ellejames.com

ALSO BY ELLE JAMES

Brotherhood Protectors Series

Montana SEAL (#1)

Bride Protector SEAL (#2)

Montana D-Force (#3)

Cowboy D-Force (#4)

Montana Ranger (#5)

Montana Dog Soldier (#6)

Montana SEAL Daddy (#7)

Montana Ranger's Wedding Vow (#8)

Montana SEAL Undercover Daddy (#9)

Cape Cod SEAL Rescue (#10)

Montana SEAL Friendly Fire (#11)

Montana SEAL's Bride (#12) TBD

Montana Rescue

Hot SEAL, Salty Dog

Hearts & Heroes Series

Wyatt's War (#1)

Mack's Witness (#2)

Ronin's Return (#3)

Sam's Surrender (#4)

Mission: Six

One Intrepid SEAL

Two Dauntless Hearts

Three Courageous Words

Four Relentless Days

Five Ways to Surrender

Six Minutes to Midnight

Take No Prisoners Series

SEAL's Honor (#1)

SEAL's Ultimate Challenge (#1.5)

SEAL'S Desire (#2)

SEAL's Embrace (#3)

SEAL's Obsession (#4)

SEAL's Proposal (#5)

SEAL's Seduction (#6)

SEAL'S Defiance (#7)

SEAL's Deception (#8)

SEAL's Deliverance (#9)

SEAL's Ultimate Challenge (#10)

Ballistic Cowboy

Hot Combat (#1)

Hot Target (#2)

Hot Zone (#3)

Hot Velocity (#4)

Texas Billionaire Club

Tarzan & Janine (#1)

Something To Talk About (#2)

Who's Your Daddy (#3)

Love & War (#4)

Hellfire Series

Hellfire, Texas (#1)

Justice Burning (#2)

Smoldering Desire (#3) TBD

Up in Flames (#4) TBD

Hellfire in High Heels (#5) TBD

Cajun Magic Mystery Series

Voodoo on the Bayou (#1)

Voodoo for Two (#2)

Deja Voodoo (#3)

Cajun Magic Mysteries Books 1-3

Billionaire Online Dating Service

The Billionaire Husband Test (#1)

The Billionaire Cinderella Test (#2)

The Billionaire Bride Test (#3) TBD

The Billionaire Matchmaker Test (#4) TBD

SEAL Of My Own

Navy SEAL Survival

Navy SEAL Captive

Navy SEAL To Die For

Navy SEAL Six Pack

Devil's Shroud Series

Deadly Reckoning (#1)

Deadly Engagement (#2)

Deadly Liaisons (#3)

Deadly Allure (#4)

Deadly Obsession (#5)

Deadly Fall (#6)

Covert Cowboys Inc Series

Triggered (#1)

Taking Aim (#2)

Bodyguard Under Fire (#3)

Cowboy Resurrected (#4)

Navy SEAL Justice (#5)

Navy SEAL Newlywed (#6)

High Country Hideout (#7)

Clandestine Christmas (#8)

Thunder Horse Series

Hostage to Thunder Horse (#1)

Thunder Horse Heritage (#2)

Thunder Horse Redemption (#3)

Christmas at Thunder Horse Ranch (#4)

Demon Series

Hot Demon Nights (#1)

Demon's Embrace (#2)

Tempting the Demon (#3)

Lords of the Underworld

Witch's Initiation (#1)

Witch's Seduction (#2)

The Witch's Desire (#3)

Possessing the Witch (#4)

Stealth Operations Specialists (SOS)

Nick of Time

Alaskan Fantasy

Blown Away

Warrior's Conquest

Rogues

Enslaved by the Viking Short Story

Conquests

Smokin' Hot Firemen

Love on the Rocks

Protecting the Colton Bride

Heir to Murder

Secret Service Rescue

High Octane Heroes

Haunted

Engaged with the Boss

Cowboy Brigade

Time Raiders: The Whisper

Bundle of Trouble

Killer Body

Operation XOXO

An Unexpected Clue

Baby Bling

Under Suspicion, With Child

Texas-Size Secrets

Cowboy Sanctuary

Lakota Baby

Dakota Meltdown

Beneath the Texas Moon

Made in the USA
Las Vegas, NV
09 November 2021